Bristol Short Story Prize Anthology

Volume Thirteen

tangent
books

Bristol Short Story Prize Anthology Volume 13

First published 2020 by Tangent Books

Tangent Books, Unit 5.16 Paintworks
Bristol, BS4 3EH
0117 972 0645
www.tangentbooks.co.uk

Email: richard@tangentbooks.co.uk

ISBN: 9781910089965

Cover designed by Roisin Oakley
www.roisinoakley.com

Layout designed by Dave Oakley, Arnos Design
www.arnosdesign.co.uk

Printed and bound by Hobbs the Printers Ltd., Brunel Rd., Totton
Hampshire, SO40 3 WX
www.hobbs.uk.com

A CIP catalogue record for this book is available from the British Library

www.tangentbooks.co.uk

www.bristolprize.co.uk

Contents

Introduction

I t is an honour to present the 13th Bristol Short Story Prize anthology. The breadth of settings, experiences, characters and imaginative creations submitted to this year's competition was truly astounding, particularly bearing in mind how dominant the global pandemic must have been in writers' minds in March and April, as our entry deadline approached.

From historical tales to dystopian futures, this year's entries kept us enthralled throughout the reading and judging process.

The top three prize-winning stories reflect the variety of the submissions: Stephen Narain's illuminating, witty and irresistible story of friendship, power, home and much more, *What In Me Is Dark, Illumine*, is awarded first prize . In taking second prize, Tehila Lieberman's powerful *Bedtime Story*, with its haunting child narrator, reminds us that "The land is full of stories if you listen". Our third prize winner for 2020 is Faiza Hasan's, *A Tapestry of Flowers*, a thought-provoking meditation on seeking out hope in the most acute situation. All three stories encapsulate what binds the collection together – the existence of a deeply rooted, unshakeable humanity, even in extreme circumstances.

It wouldn't have been possible to produce this collection without the support and commitment of many people during what has been such an uncertain and challenging few months. Particular thanks are owed to our readers and judges who were so adaptable to the changing circumstances and whose dedication ensured that we were able to stick to our original schedule.

Big thanks, also, to Chris Hill and Jonathan Ward, tutors on the Illustration degree course at the University of the West of England here in Bristol. Chris and Jonathan's ingenuity ensured we were able to run our anthology cover design project as usual and the eye-catching design of this year's collection is the work of recent graduate, Roisin Oakley.

And warm thanks to Professors Helen Fulton and Mary Luckhurst of the University of Bristol, who have enabled us to launch an exciting collaboration with the University's new MA in Creative Writing.

We hope you enjoy these 20 fantastic stories as much as we have. Many congratulations to the writers who have been selected and to all those who entered this year's competition from around the world. We are deeply indebted to you all for submitting your work to us during this most heightened of times.

Joe Melia, *Bristol Short Story Prize Co-ordinator*

1st Prize
Stephen Narain

Stephen Narain was raised in Freeport, Bahamas by Guyanese parents and moved to Miami at seventeen. He earned an AB in English from Harvard University and an MFA in Fiction from the Iowa Writers' Workshop, where he won a Soros New American Fellowship. Stephen is the recipient of the Small Axe Fiction Prize, the Alice Yard Prize for Art Writing, and the American Civil Liberties Union's National Youth Activist Scholarship for work assisting attorneys defending the First Amendment. In 2012, the Bocas Lit Fest selected Stephen for its New Talent Showcase, spotlighting promising Caribbean writers. He lives in Orlando, Florida.

What In Me Is Dark, Illumine

Come, comrade stargazer.
Look at the sky I told you I had seen.
The glittering seeds that germinate in darkness.
And the planet in my hand's revolving wheel.
And the planet in my breast and in my head
and in my dream and in my furious blood.
Let me rise up wherever he may fall.
I am no soldier hunting in a jungle.
I am this poem like a sacrifice.

– Martin Carter, *Poems of Resistance
from British Guiana* (1954)

The Revolutionary did not look like a "Revolutionary." Didn't possess Che Guevara's patchy beard. Fidel Castro's lion eyes. Brother was shaped like a cricket player. Very slender. Very strong. Brother spoke in Aristotelian paragraphs, his voice calm, even at its crescendo. How did he manage this, this balance of sense and sensibility? This Walter Rodney. This "Brother Wally." This Comrade Stargazer. The Revolutionary didn't wear bell-bottoms. He wore an economics professor's spring semester khakis, John-the-Baptist sandals, and a white shirt-jac stained beneath the armpits. His too-serious face was framed by horn-rimmed spectacles. His Afro was substantial enough to make its point, yet too tame for 1978. Style, his Afro suggested, was secondary to something else. But what? Tulsi turned to Anand, his best friend his whole life, and wanted to whisper in his ear that the two of them – the Sweetboy and the Revolutionary – shared the same two values, the latter admittedly ineffable, but in reverse. Anand was listening too hard; his listening was a performance. Tulsi could tell. This is love: knowing when your friend is putting on and growing frustrated by all that pretense. The unnecessary carnival. Quarter to nine. Tulsi tapped his toes. Bit his thumbnail. Begged Lord Ganesha to bring this meeting – and all its causes – to a swift, Aristotelian dénouement.

They had assembled in Gobin's bottom house. Three weeks prior, a Working People's gathering in New Amsterdam had been raided by the Dictator's sycophants, a rebel arrested, accused of vandalizing a ministry office when six alibis – his wife, pregnant, included – had testified the comrade was home feeding his child. Tulsi told Anand they ought to be cautious. They should go to Ling's. To the cricket ground. But Anand kissed his teeth, in his way, and made it clear that he wanted Tulsi to *see* something, to *feel* something before he boarded that plane back to Toronto to read all those books that were separating him from these men. Tulsi watched the two dozen comrades – workers he had spent his whole life hellbent on not becoming. Men who worked in the bauxite mines and on the sugar estates, men who wore sacks beneath their eyes, men who smelled of salt and El Dorado rum, which they nursed while the Revolutionary preached.

"But Brother Wally!" the big-skin man in front of him interjected.

"Comrade Beckles," the Revolutionary said.

"Alright. Whole time, eh? Steadysteady you ah go on bout how we can mek it on we own business, dat we can build tings fuh weself. But hear me good, nuh? We have dis jackass breathing over we. Figure me dis. How we gonna cause dem bigbig change you ah preach bout when we mouth always muzzle by de food we eating fuh live?"

The Revolutionary braced his backside against the greenheart table. He took a 750 milliliter bottle of 15-year and asked Comrade Beckles for his empty glass.

"Watch this glass," the Revolutionary said.

He poured the El Dorado into the glass until it flowed onto the concrete ground.

Tulsi thought of the 23rd Psalm.

"Gosh, boy, Wally. Is wha really you ah try prove so?"

"Beckles, sometimes we brain so full up dat we can't let new possibilities in."

"Alright. You make yuh point," Beckles said, genuinely mourning the wasted spirit.

"How shall we empty our cups?" the Revolutionary asked.

Silently, Tulsi sucked his teeth. A sandfly was feeding from his calf. He murdered it.

When a man performs goodness so well – so completely – what are his vices?

This was the question Tulsi asked Anand on their walk home, kiskadees shrieking, involved in their own protest against insignificance. The evening prior, Anand and Shirley were lazing on his verandah when Anand tossed a book from his satchel on Tulsi's lap.

How Europe Underdeveloped Africa.

On the cover, white hands tearing a red continent shaped like a heartbreak.

You know Brother Wally does write books?

Anand asked the question like he were the Revolutionary's rishi. He, Ganesha. The Revolutionary, Vyasa. Shirley was watching how Tulsi handled the book. He disliked the cover. Something too simple about it. Who was the artist? Was he from Europe? Had he been to Africa? Shirley might have judged him if he did not perform interest, and he wanted Shirley to think he was interested, though he was not.

I hear he's a genius, Shirley had said.

Tulsi had gone to the meeting to decide if her suspicion was true.

In 1977, Tulsi received a Commonwealth Scholarship to study Latin American literature at the University of Toronto. For a Guyanese boy with middle-class roots, there are many useless things you can study. Latin American literature is up there with Folklore & Mythology. But how could he express his love for Gabriel García Márquez? How might he describe to the world that feeling of *feeling* a book inside oneself so wholly, so deeply, so unconditionally? How could he describe the dignity and clarity he derived from the exchange? The same dignity and clarity the Working People had been denied by Cain. Were you not meant to pursue the path that made you tremble and laugh and sweat when you made your first step?

The Friday evening after the meeting, Anand and Bucket and Fineman and Fatman and Shirley were walking home from Glory's Cinema. Shirley and her brother Bucket – so named because his head was indeed shaped like a bucket, Fineman named Fineman because he was fat, Fatman named Fatman because he was not – walked ahead of

Anand and Tulsi, the two friends lamenting the brevity of life. Tulsi took in his friend. Anand had gained twenty pounds, solid muscle. He spent the past year drinking milk, lifting weights. He looked like one of those dancers, bred in Brooklyn, from "Saturday Night Fever." He looked like a coolie John Travolta. He wore cream bell-bottoms and a too-tight shirt unbuttoned near the navel. He managed to cultivate a hairstyle as close to an Afro that a human being of Indian origin could possibly present to the August street.

"Boy, it's why you showing off your body so?" Tulsi asked. "You looking like you have something to prove?"

"Comrade, you know I making the world better with alla dis sweetness."

"Call me anything, brother. But I ain't no comrade."

Anand looked hurt, and Tulsi wanted to hurt him, ever so slightly. Hurt him into a greater sense of responsibility. Hurt him away from his pretenses. Break his mask.

Anand and his friends were off to Ling's for lo mein and garlic prawns.

"Come, nuh?" Anand asked. "I mean, what waiting for you home? Shakespeare? What Shakespeare have on Shirley Persaud?"

How we would miss her. This girl he wished would fly back with him to Toronto, this girl who had no interest in leaving Georgetown or her family, who had no interest in snow or libraries, a girl who was one with that place, who sang when she spoke, who danced when she walked, who worked scooping ice cream in her daddy's parlor and was content.

"I should go back," Tulsi said.

"It's alright," Anand said. "I know you good. What you think of dat book, eh?"

But Tulsi had not read Brother Wally's history. The street divided. Tulsi said goodbye to his friend – too abruptly, he knew, the question left fluttering in the night air like a tired butterfly.

The next day, he, Shirley, and Anand went to his Uncle Ganesha's house to pay respect to Mother Durga, the goddess of war.

"Praise God you so maga," Anand said. "Climb on, but hold tight. Shirley already there. If we don't speed, we gon be late!"

Anand swooshed left, swerved right at least ten times as he towed him. Cars honked. Girls laughed. Anand flexed his bicep at the stop sign.

"Eh, boy, I ain't get tow in a while," Tulsi said. "Take it easy, nuh?! You driving tootoo wild!"

Anand kissed his teeth. They flew into the wrong side of the city. Broken houses neighboring broken houses. Clotheslines hanging from metal crosses on Calvary. Chickens danced and clucked, swaggering more proudly than their reputations. Tulsi searched for the house on Cuffy Road. Searched for the jandi flags. Inhaled hard for the scent of incense and camphor and cloves.

Tulsi hopped off the bicycle, and Anand chained it to the wrought iron gates.

The puja was just beginning. The courtyard buzzing, believers arranging the last of the oleanders onto iron plates. Women lighting votives. Fellows testing drums. Sitar music started. Four girls, shalwars grazing the ground, carried Mother Durga on a bamboo dais. Her ten arms clutched weapons like arrows and scimitars and swords. Shirley led the procession, the kohl lining her eyes changing her citizenship: she became Egyptian. The skin peeking out from the red silk of her costume was the color of sapodillas that just fell from their tree.

During Uncle Ganesha's sermon, his own daddy's words streamed into his soul like breeze.

Son, plentyplenty fella sit down like saint whole day and chant dis and talk fatfat, but ask dem fuh actually take a bullet for them brother, eh? Ask them to give the shirt off their own back. Suddenly pussycat claw they throat. Me forget if it was Jesus or Buddha or Allah who say: "Show me yuh deeds. Show me yuh wuk." Hear me good, soon: me don't worship no god. What I worship is work.

Twilight confuddled the sky. Old ladies brought out the fried pholourie in big baskets, their daughters and granddaughters behind them with tamarind chutney, with mango achaar. Pandit Ganesha summoned all the children to his feet. He wrapped a knock-kneed boy in his arms, the little boy's eyes so wide he might as well have been glimpsing Jupiter. Tulsi left Anand with his cousins to stand by the fire with Shirley, frying mithai in hot oil.

"Y'all ready fuh hear dis story bout Mother Durga?" Uncle Ganesha asked.

The children – two dozen lotuses – their knees touching, placed index fingers on their lips, shushed their brothers, tugged their earlobes.

"Alright," Uncle Ganesha started. "Longlongtime ago, there was a demon – half man, half buffalo – who wreak all kinda havoc pon dis world. No god nor goddess could kill he. He was scampish and skillful, and dem two tings together, man, is a dangerous, dangerous pair. Dis demon mash up a whole heap of gods – like dis fella conscience evaporate in the sky. One day, Lord Vishnu... man, he couldn't take it no more. He get madmadmad, you hear me? Madmad like when a brother learn he own blood wanna kill he. That kinda feeling. Like the sun betray he, like he ain't know if de earth gonna fall out from under he foot. One bigbig beam of light start pouring outta he mouth and, hear dis, nuh?! Light start pouring outta alla de mouths of every god the demon defeat and, from this light, a woman was born, and dis woman name Mother Durga.

"Now, lemme give y'all de skinny pon de deal, eh? Mother Durga was no pushover. She wasn't bowing down to any fool. Lady was a brick house. *A BRICK HOUSE!* All de gods, see: they donate they weapons – that's how come she ten hands get full up so. Now, when the demon checking out Mother Durga, he getting real frighten. I mean he never see a woman cocky so. Mother sitting on top of a lion! She start galloping straight toward the demon, and de demon think he could mash she up still, but, see, he ain't know the force of her will. Mother Durga slay he whole army like snap, and the demon pride get bust up. *He* change into a lion; Mother chop of he head. Change into a swordsman; Mother pull out she bow. The demon madmadmad now! How a *woman* could beat he, eh?! A *woman*?! The demon change into something truly wild… what he turn into, darlings?"

"A BUFFALO?!" the children screamed, though they'd heard this story ten thousand times before.

"Do you think Mother was scared?" Uncle Ganesha asked.

"NAHHH!" the children screamed.

"Righteous ting! Mother was cool. Calm. Collected. Just like Miss Diana Ross. De buffalo start charging and Mother do something a lil bit different dis time. She stop. Stare straight into the demon eye. Study what evil *look* like. Record its shape. Its colors. She *breathe.* Squint she two eye, open she third, reach for a simple, shiny trident, aim, steady – easy – like Arjuna fighting a battle he don't really wanna fight at all. Mother surrender. Release. And do you think Mother made the final shot, my children?"

The children clapped their hands. They smiled.

"Yes, my darlings. The demon's head was severed. But only because Mother look at what no one dare look at ever before. I reckon Mother was frighten. But she look. Still. And what she learn? Dat's above my pay scale, darlings. But if I gotta guess, children, it might be something like this: Evil ain't evil at all. Evil just a lesson waiting on the other side of fear."

It was a forty-five minute walk from Uncle Ganesha's house to their homes in the heart of Georgetown. It was Saturday, the city Dutch and damp, the night sky sluggish, a prologue to the summer rain. Shirley and he walked as one, Anand rolling his bicycle beside them. Palm trees were black, Amazonian. Asphalt even blacker than the pitch of its origin. The fat Queen Victoria was still missing her marble nose. A fellow was quarreling with a rival in front of a tie-dye lorry. Mad Mr. Chin still fetched peanuts atop his head – you had to give the fellow marks for assiduousness – running up to Buicks and Bedfords when they stopped at the light, calling on passengers, exchanging peanuts for coins with the grace of Double Nought Seven.

The Dictator had banned wheat flower. Labeled dates and apples "imperialist." Tulsi worried for his mummy, her arms leaner, more sinewy – too muscular for a woman who worshiped sweets the way his daddy worshiped work. She'd pound rice with a mortar and pestle just to make flour for roti.

You ah tell me, she sang. *Dat me nuh have nothing better fuh do with me time? Dat Burnham is a dolt, you hear me? You watch. One day me papers gonna come and boom! Mohini Ramkissoon gone! You hear me?! Gone! Me gonna find my way to America by hook or by crook and make all de roti me want.*

Tulsi was his mummy's son. He could care less for Guyana's politricks.

He was committed to the food of art, to the art of food: to grandeur, to excess, to sharing callaloo, to perfecting the subtlest of flavors. And this was the quality of the government Tulsi disdained the most: its clear lack of appreciation for the differences between a dahl made from channa and one made from split yellow peas.

"De truth," Anand said, turning the corner. "Is dat we dealing with the lesser of fifty evils. Don't think I naïve. You think I believe everything Brother Wally say? Nah. The 10,000 foot-rule. Pandit Ganesha teach me dat. Fly above the world. Look at what is what. I know dis fella can't be Black Jesus. Besides, every messiah have he sin. But at least Brother Wally – let's assume… true, dat's a dangerous ting… to assume – but let's assume dat all that history-learning, all that teaching, all that preaching, dat de way he look at he wife, that the gentleness of he eyes, and alla that genius…"

"He is a genius… " Tulsi said.

"Well, then, alla dat genius… let's just assume that we can hope that, if he gain power, at least he ain't gonna forget that he daddy was a tailor who give him the shirt he mend heself."

"He ain't gon last," Shirley said from nowhere.

And they both knew exactly what she meant.

They walked her up to her house, waved at her parents.

"Who I sorry for is he pickney," Shirley said. "When the Demon kill dat man, what his wife s'posed to say to she child?"

To progress, Pandit Ganesha said, *you can't always be kind. You can't always sit down and expect God to come to you side. Sometime a demon might rub up next to you; sometime that demon might be your own kin. Nah, boy. Sometimes you have to flip. You ain't know Mother Kali? You ain't know how she does run off? Man, when she start you ain't want be fifty miles too close to she madness. Lady chop of you head if you get in she way.*

Tulsi sat on the verandah with his family, his mummy nibbling on contraband dates. She used that carnival of misery, that festival of guns to her advantage: to laugh more loudly. *If Burnham could kill you, you might as well speak the words on your mind.* His daddy's belly was full. Sweet gilbaka curry, potato roti, three kinds of dahl. He told them he ate at the puja. All he wanted was tea. Extra cream.

He knew they were proud of him. You just know those things – can't fake it. They didn't mind that he was studying madmen: Márquez and Borges and Carpentier. They didn't understand their only child, but they loved what they didn't understand, and he loved them for loving what they didn't understand, and this was love: allowing your child back into the circle even when he risked becoming the Prodigal Son.

Tulsi loved his friends in Toronto, even though they could not understand the texture of where he was from. They believed he lived in some complicated paradise, and he allowed them to speak so he could know what they thought.

He refused every spliff he was offered.

I mean, my man, you're telling me, you don't smoke the ganja every day?

Michel was like a genial bear, heavy-footed, but well-meaning. The first time he met Michel's girlfriend, Clémence, he wondered what the Caribbean sun would do to her skin.

Where are you from?, she asked him in her rhythm: raspy, Québécois.

Guyana, he said and felt peculiar pronouncing the country like a mantra.

Ghana?, Clémence asked.

No. Guyana, Tulsi repeated. *Ghana, West Africa. Guyana, South America.*

Clémence searched the room for an atlas.

West of Suriname, Tulsi explained only to realize that explanation likely did not help her confusion. *Brazil*, he decided. *North of Brazil.*

But it's like Jamaica, no?!, Michel asked, inhaling his spliff, exhaling an O in the air. *I mean you talk like the Bob Marley.*

Michel had the tendency to place a definite article in front of the names of men he believed were destined for Zion.

Yes, Tulsi surrendered. He had tossed and turned the night before. *Imagine Jamaica, in South America.*

Like how Québec is a French country in Canada?, Michel.

Oui, Tulsi said, lifting the coffee mug to his lips.

"Daddy," he said out of nowhere.

"Yes, comrade."

"Stop!"

"I have a question. Dis Rodney? What you think of him?"

"I dunno, boy. You know yuh daddy mind he own business. He don't get mix up in dem sorta tings."

"Seem bright," his mummy say. "Good looking."

"Anand invite me to a rally Friday. You think I should go?"

"Might do you some good," his daddy said. "Just stay on the fringe. Run like hell when shit start to fly."

His mummy didn't laugh.

"Do you *want* to go?" she asked.

No, he thought.

"No," he said. "But Anand might be mad."

"Sweetheart, you don't know Anand figure dat he best friend buy a one-way ticket to Mars?"

His mummy was right. When Tulsi explained he'd not be going to the rally, Anand said he figured as much. Tulsi had two weeks left in

Guyana.

"Stay with your girl," Anand said. "You ain't remember what Brother Marcus say? 'You can leave life right now, let that determine what you do and say and think.'"

Tulsi smiled. When he had given Anand back the copy of *How Europe Underdeveloped Africa*, Tulsi gave Anand a slim volume of the *Meditations of Marcus Aurelius*. Anand said it sounded like that Roman had really been burned by life.

"I teaching you to dance. Tonight!" Shirley said the afternoon of the rally. "I mean you a shame. To your country. To the Caribbean. Come home. Tonight."

"But Uncle Vishnu?"

"Daddy know what is what. You know he like you real bad. Call you a gentleman."

They watched Anand walk down the road, and a part of Tulsi walked with him. He didn't want to look at her, not just then, and she knew why.

"Just come, boy. I get that Bee Gees vinyl! Groovy ting! We lime on de verandah. Tonight, I don't think it supposed to rain."

The lessons didn't last too long.

"How a man can live in Guyana his *whole life* and move like a chicken getting ready to die?"

"I dat bad?"

"Boy, whatever you doing beyond apology. Stop. Let we sit down."

She pulled him by the thumb and led him to the greenheart swing on her verandah. Lit the kerosene lamp. Rubbed lemon and eucalyptus on his arms to repel the sandflies.

With the Bee Gees silent, the night could sing.

"You know that Third Eye Pandit Ganesha steady talking about?

When you open it, you know what I realize? You can't *think* so much. Darling, that's why you can't dance as good as I know you can. You always *thinking* so much! Holding your cards so close to that chest, you never just let yourself play. Your pride is your brain – that's the mark of you, you think. But, darling, I like you for more than your brain."

"For what?"

"For one, I dunno? I like looking at you."

Tulsi had long thought of his corporeality as some ill-equipped vessel to hold astral light.

"'Oh, that this too solid flesh would melt,'" he said like somebody's granddaddy.

"Hamlet, that madass," Shirley said. "First soliloquy. Don't think I wasn't listening that day."

"I know you was listening. That's why I want you come with me one day."

"Where? To Canada? You fall on yuh head. Just cause I know my Shakespeare don't mean I gonna leave my Guyana."

"That's not what I meant."

"Then what did you mean? I ain't gonna say the brutal thing like I think you think you too good for we."

"You just said it."

"But, I brighter than that, comrade. Fact is you here with me and these sandflies on this same here verandah. And you here with Anand. And you love us, and we love you, and, sorry, but dat ain't gon change."

"I coming back."

"God say don't lie. You ain't coming back, darling. You gonna stay. Or fly to America. Boy, you gonna flyyy! I know you. What's that school you steady running on about? That Princeton. That Princeton gonna catch you. Dat sound like de kinda place people like you does go." She laughed. "My prince. At Princeton."

"And you wouldn't come?"

Shirley sighed.

"My Tulsi. Same Tulsi. So smart and so slow. Darling, ain't you know? Some roads just don't meet."

2nd Prize
Tehila Lieberman

Tehila Lieberman's debut short story collection, *Venus in the Afternoon*, received the Katherine Anne Porter Prize in Short Fiction and was published by UNT Press. Individual stories have been awarded the Stanley Elkin Memorial Prize and the Rick DeMarinis Short Fiction Award and have appeared in many literary journals. Tehila's non-fiction has appeared in Salon.com and in several *Travelers' Tales Guides* anthologies and has been nominated for a Pushcart Prize. Originally from New York, Tehila lives in Cambridge, Massachusetts where she consults as a writing coach for Harvard Business School. She is completing final revisions on a first novel entitled, *The Last Holy Man.*

Bedtime Story

There is a bedtime story Mama Angel used to tell me. It was when the first people were coming in their wagons across the huge empty land. Of course, Mama Angel says it wasn't empty. The hills and forests were full of eyes and animals.

No one noticed when the little girl fell out of the wagon as the horses pulled it up up up between the trees. The mama was holding the reins, the men were sleeping like sacks of potatoes. The wagon went up up up trying to not get stuck in the tree roots or mud. It creaked and squawked on the uneven ground so that the mama didn't hear the light thump as the girl fell into a bed of leaves.

Only a starling saw the girl. A starling that had lost its flock. When she would get up to that part, Mama Angel would stop and say – "A flock of starlings is called a murmuration," and the two of us would say it a few times together – murmuration. Mama Angel said it sounded like a prayer.

I stop talking because I can hear Mama's voice and my voice saying "murmuration".

"And then what happened?" Mama Witch asks me.

"Well – " I begin to say. Because Mama told it to me so many times,

I know it by heart. "The starling flew in front of the baby's face but just out of reach so the baby chased it crawling so fast, she didn't notice the jab of a twig on its knee or the many things that were alive on the forest floor. The starling stopped in front of a small cave and the baby crawled up to the mouth of the cave and there inside a humongous stuffed animal opened its eyes and she giggled. "Beah," she said and the bear rolled onto its side to get a better look at the furless cub.

"It was cold and the baby was tired so she crawled up to the bear and squeezed between the baby bears, up against the mama bear's furry side and fell asleep."

Mama Witch is watching me with big big eyes and I keep going.

"Now the baby had everything she needed and a mama who loved her so so much and showed her how to fish with her mouth and how to climb trees so fast and the baby was happy. Then one day, some people came into the woods. It was all men. The Indians had stolen the baby's mama but the papa came back to find her. The baby who was now a little girl watched him from the cave and tried to call out to him but all that came out were some clacking sounds and a growl and her papa walked backwards out of the woods and she never saw him ever again."

When I finish the story, Mama Witch says, "Crazy story. Who teaches a child so much tragedy?"

Daddy shakes his head. "It's a story about life, survival, the randomness of loss." Daddy always has his head stuck in books and he says big words no one understands.

Mama Witch looks at Papa and says – "Boy, you two must have been quite the pair."

In my head, I call her "Mama Witch" because she came and Mama disappeared right over the bridge on the Kanawha River. Daddy says that's a mixed up order. That mama flew off the bridge to be an angel and then when he and I were too sad to even eat any breakfast – she – an old friend of his from 100 years ago (she doesn't look that old) who was living in Rurope came back and found him all broken.

When I talk to her, Papa wants me to call Mama Witch Mama 2 but I call her Judy. I don't like Judy because with every day that she lives with us, a day with Mama Angel falls out of the part of my head where I remember things.

At school, just before summer, I ask my teacher Miss Rose, where is Rurope? She looks at me funny and says, come. And she walks me over to the big spinning ball with the whole world drawn on it and tiny tiny words.

"Is it close?"

"No, it's not that close," and she takes her finger and points at where we are and says an airplane would fly like this to Europe and her finger moves across a big blue ocean.

"Why?" Miss Rose asks me "Why do you want to know?"

"Bad people come from Rurope," I say and she looks at me funny. "What bad people?" she says. But I don't answer.

She tilts her head at me and says, "Do you mean Nazis? Are you folks Jewish?" I don't know what that is and so I shrug and walk away.

Sometimes Mama Witch reads to me. She only picks stories with happy endings but it makes me sad because it hides the sad things that can happen. Daddy says even the sadness has beauty and Mama Witch says, "What are you on?"

Like every summer since I was in Mommy's belly, when school ends we drive to the big green lake but now Daddy is bringing Mama Witch and she is going to sleep where Mama Angel used to sleep. I think the lake is where Mama Angel's ghost will come to visit because Daddy says she loved it so much – the lake with the chirping frogs. It seems like we are driving forever, And I am happy and also sad. Last year Mama Angel was sitting in the front of the car and she and Daddy were singing loud to a song on the radio. Something down to Yasgar's farm.

"What's so special about Yasgar's farm?" I asked. "What kind of animals does it have?" And they both laughed. I didn't know what was funny but I laughed with them.

Finally we stop driving. We are at the cabin with the big big lake and rowboats bobbing up and down and those pointy canoes they call kayaks.

The first day mama would help Daddy take all the suitcases in and then she would take me to the store in town and I would pick out a tire tube and a raft that was funner than the old ones I had. I loved the animal rafts and last year I stretched out and closed my eyes and wiggled my toes in the sun on a big panda lying on his back taking a cool nap. Last year Mama chose a tube that was a round piece of pineapple with a palm tree growing out it.

"How cool is this?" she said when she found it.

And we'd come back to the cabin with our floating toys and Daddy would blow them up, making his face so red, mama would hold her belly laughing. And Mama and I would take them down to the water and float away. "Listen to the silence," Mama Angel would say, but that would make me confused because it was louder than at home with the burping of a gazillion frogs and bugs buzzing and birds talking to each other and the shishishing of the water all around us. The best part would be when Mama Angel would start to sing a song I didn't know and then she'd teach it to me.

Or she'd tell me a story about a bird that flew low over us. That bird is a spirit, she would say. It once was a little Indian girl who knew a lot about the land.

Last year mama was in the middle of telling me a story when she stopped and put her hand over her eyes. "Look," she said and I put my hand over my eyes like Mama and far far away on the other side of the lake there was a bear and three little cubs.

"So beautiful," Mama whispers.

"So beautiful," I say though they are so small I can hardly see them so I imagine the big brown bear in the bedtime story guarding the cubs so that they can drink.

During the day I try to talk to Mama's ghost. Don't be scared, I say, come closer. But then at night I hold my teddy bear close, because I'm listening for her and I'm too scared to sleep. I get so scared, I close my eyes and pray she doesn't come and then in the morning I am sorry.

Mama Angel was so beautiful and fun, everyone loved her. We'd get out of the car and be at the cabin and then poof – we were friends with the family next door on the pine tree side and on the other side where the sand stops. The kids would invite me over and we'd splash all day and have races in the water. When the light turned yellow and blue, we'd catch fireflies in jars that mama found under the sink.

This time the cabin on the pine tree side had us over for a fun barbecue, but we don't see the family on the right a lot. Early early in the morning a big man leaves in an ugly old car. And a tired woman who looks like the baby's grandma pushes a stroller up and down the path that is in front of the cabins and sometimes goes all the way around the lake. Daddy said she smokes like a chimney and I watch to see if the smoke comes out of her head instead of her mouth but I never see it.

And then when we are in the water and the sun is that fire color and the lake is like a big mirror filled with puffy clouds, the grandma sometimes goes indoors and we smell her cooking which doesn't smell so great.

And then when it's dark, and the big ugly man comes home, Daddy says, "I can smell the alcohol from here" and then the gramma comes outside and hands him a bottle of something. Daddy says it's beer. Daddy also says that's not the baby's grandma, it's her mama but daddys don't know everything and I don't think he's right.

They never say hello even if I stare right at them.

After everyone goes to sleep, I stay up and I read with the bright yellow head lamp Mama Angel bought me last year. And I hear them yelling and then it's like someone is throwing things at the wall.

And I hear the mama yell, "Don't you dare touch her," but the baby starts to cry and then scream.

After two nights of the same thing, I tell Daddy, "I don't like those people."

"Why?" he asks.

"They yell and yell and the baby cries and cries." I want to say and maybe the baby is getting hurt but Daddy would say I got an overactive magination like Mama, so I don't tell him that. He stays awake, waiting but nothing happens and I look outside and there's no beat up car and I say, "He's not back yet" and Daddy falls asleep.

But two nights later, I hear it again and I run to Daddy and Mama Witch's room and I push my fingers into Daddy's shoulder. Wake up wake up. And he comes out but by the time he comes to the window where I listen when things go thump against the wall, nothing is going on. Then we hear the baby crying.

Daddy looks at me and says, "The baby probably just has colic. He tells me that I had colic when I was a baby and that they used to put me on a washing machine and turn it on to calm me down. In a few months her stomach will learn how to handle food and she won't cry at all," Daddy says.

But I know it's not colic – whatever that is. The baby only cries like that when the man is there.

In the morning while they're having their yucky coffee, I hear Daddy say to Mama Witch, "That woman's going to smoke herself to death" and suddenly I think – the baby's going to get a Mama Angel too, though it's hard to imagine the grandma mama as an angel with her red face and bad bad smell.

Today I count. The grandma mama goes out 13 times to smoke and baby is alone. Then I see her, her face all red, leave and walk halfway around the lake.

She is walking a little funny and I think maybe she's going to turn into an angel today and Daddy and Mama Witch are taking showers, Daddy in the outdoor shower, Mama Witch in the bathroom which she makes so hot, the steam comes under the door. And so I walk over to their cabin where the sand runs out and I open the door quietly and go inside where it's really messy and the baby is awake just lying in her crib and she sees me and smiles and I wind up her mobile and run back to our cabin.

Sometimes I hear Daddy and Mama Witch talking and they don't know I can hear. Like right after dinner when they are doing the dishes I hear Mama Witch whisper, "Third sighting." I don't know what sighting is but I think she kind of whispered it so she didn't want me to hear and I don't ask.

She leans over to Daddy and says, "eating from the Mathews' garbage can."

Then Mama Witch looks up and sees me in the doorway and they both are quiet.

When we used to come here before Mama witch, some days Mama and me would have sleepovers in her bed. Daddy would say, Maggie, honey, please get up and mama would be lying there not sad not happy just saying to me, there are days when the gravity is so strong I can't move. What is gavity? I would ask Daddy and he would look at me so sad and say – it's the pull of the earth trying keep Mama in one place. "But she is in one place," and Daddy would nod and get teary. And then mama would say. I'm sorry baby girl. I'm sorry." Sometimes when the gavity was really bad, Mama would pull herself up to lean against the back of the bed and pull her knees in tight tight and stare at something at the end of the bed and her eyes were so scared I got scared and then Daddy would scoop me up and take me for ice cream but I would say no, we have to stay with Mama and he said the gavity would pass faster if we didn't. I don't know if that's true. I think he wanted me to not be scared and he would buy me way too much ice cream and my tummy would hurt.

Daddy says we've been here a week and have two more to go and I say the hole in my belly where I miss Mama Angel is getting bigger and his eyes get sad and he says, "Mine too, baby girl," and I watch his eyes to see if he will cry like I do but since Mama Witch came he never does.

"What if Mama fell into the river?" I say to Daddy when he is tucking me in.

"Na," he says. "Mama's wings grew out of her back the second she stepped off the bridge," and I imagine those wings with their big white feathers and I want to climb on them and fly with Mama to wherever she went.

In the morning, Daddy says Mama Witch needs something from town. "Come, Pumpkin, let's get in the car," he says, grabbing his keys and I say, "No, I want to stay here."

"C'mon," Daddy says. "We can stop at the library and get you some new books." But I shake my head and I look at them and say what Mama Angel always used to say, "The land is full of stories if you listen," and Daddy smiles a sad smile and Mama Witch shakes her head like she does whenever I say something Mama Angel used to say and he and Mama Witch put their heads together so they won't be loud and they whisper. Then Daddy says "Ok, we will let you stay here, but you can't leave the cabin until we come back."

"Ok, I say. I will be good." And they leave and I think – I'm a big girl now and I carry the breakfast dishes to the sink like I see Mama Witch do and I don't break anything. Then I hear the man's car pull into the driveway next to our cabin. It's early, I think, for him to be home and I hear the screech of their screen door and he walks into the baby's cabin. And he and grandma mama start their yelling in the middle of the day and then he slams the door and drives away with a big big screech and grandma mama comes out of the cabin walking all funny and starts to walk around the lake and the trees swallow her up.

I'm a big girl now, I tell myself and when I can't see the grandma mama anymore, I tiptoe next door and go in and the baby smiles at me. I pick her up and we go out the back door to where Mama used to say the trees kiss the cabins.

The baby is heavy. I thought she would feel like my Crissy doll but when I hold her my arms begin to hurt and I have to tell myself, I'm a big girl and my arms are going to get big and strong.

I walk into the woods and count my steps because I don't have any breadcrumbs. One two three four. I hit twenty and I don't know what comes next so I do the alphabet that Miss Rose taught us and I showed off to Daddy and Mama Witch. A, B, C, D. In front of me I see some big rocks that look like they falled from the mountain. They point up and lean on each other like they are the roof of a house. I crouch down and put the baby inside and I put her pacifier that is tied to her shirt in her mouth and I say, be good, baby girl. You will have a happy life here, little girl. And then I hear something behind me and suddenly I am scared but I don't run. I count my way out of the woods.

When I come out there is no one around. Daddy and Mama Witch are still in town and I see the grandma mama coming back from her walk around the lake and she is puffing smoke like a choo choo train and then she goes in the cabin and then she is screaming just as Daddy and Mama Witch's car comes down the road and into the driveway. And Mama Witch runs into grandma mama's house and Daddy is talking to some of the other men who have run up to the cabin. Then there are sirens and police cars like in the shows Daddy watches on television. Mama Witch takes my hand and we walk all around looking for the baby.

Mama Angel must have whispered something to Daddy because he comes up to where we are and crouches down and looks right at me. What have you done, baby girl? What did you do?

And I want to tell him but Mama Witch is standing right there and looking at me very funny. She is a witch and soon I feel her eyes burning into mine and I think she's going to go through my eyes and into my head and then her face changes and she looks like she just saw something very scary in my head and she says Oh God and begins to run into the woods. A few minutes later the policemen are running into the woods and Daddy starts to cry and I think, finally. Finally he is missing Mama Angel. And then a policeman is talking to Daddy and

Mama Witch comes out of the woods and her arms are empty and she comes up to where I am and crouches down. And tells me that if I don't tell her where I put the baby, they will think Daddy isn't a good daddy because they left me alone and I could get the baby killed. "Eaten," she said. I shake my head, no no, because even if she's a witch, she doesn't know everything. And then a policemen is talking to me and asking me questions but I don't say a word. I don't move. The woods are big, I think. And maybe all the polices won't find the baby before the Mama bear. Daddy is trying to talk to me and I sit and don't move. I try not to blink. I just stare ahead and I feel closer than ever to Mama Angel because I'm a big girl now and I'm beginning to understand that sometimes the world is all wrong and you need to stay very still and go inside the gavity. Deep, deep, deep inside.

3rd Prize

Faiza Hasan

Faiza Hasan has an MSt in Creative Writing from Cambridge University, and an MA in Journalism from Stanford University, USA. She has worked as a journalist in Pakistan and the US. Her short stories have been longlisted for *The Guardian* BAME Short Story Prize, *Harpers Bazaar*, San Miguel Writers' Conference, White Review, and Glimmer Train. She has also been a general contributor at the prestigious Bread Loaf Writers' Conference in the USA. She lives in Berkshire with her husband, boys, and dog, Tintin. She is currently working on her first novel.

A Tapestry of Flowers

The brown, burlap sack sits like a large, squat toad on his doorstep. Gul Khan inhales sharply before looking around the empty street, but the hazy smoke rising from breakfast fires around his neighbourhood conceal him from curious eyes. The only witnesses are the misty, blue mountains surrounding his valley and they are, he knows, indifferent to the lives of men. He wants to close the door and go back to bed, but the thick, crisscrossing scars on his back twinge with warning. His shoulders slump with defeat as he bends down and grabs the sack by its scratchy hemp rope, his stiff, old shoulders creaking in protest as he drags it inside.

Dawn paints the mud packed courtyard in shades of rose and gold, and for a few minutes at least, the small space is cloaked in beauty. A tall mulberry tree with its emerald leaves and dangling unripe fruit, like tiny pale worms, glows in the middle of the enclosure. It is all wasted on Gul Khan, whose attention is transfixed by the sack, the fourth delivery this year. He drags it past the tree, through the kitchen into his bedroom and turns the light on. The bare bulb swings from a frayed electric cord casting dark, swaying shadows against the peeling walls, like the *jinns* of his childhood nightmares. Sometimes, late at night, when he is firmly in thrall of the opium, the *jinns* crawl up his bedroom walls to leer at him from the ceiling. He lays his heart open to them, his every secret wish, every desire laid bare. They listen quietly when he cries fat, guilty tears that seep from the corner of eyes into his pillow. But other nights, especially when the wind howls through the narrow streets of his village like a maddened beast, he hears them talk back. And their voices are not gentle or kind.

"Coward," they hiss.

Gul Khan heaves the bundle onto his bed. Next to it is an ancient Singer sewing machine, a relic inherited from his grandfather who had been a Tailor Master in the British army. He pulls out a dented tin chest from under the machine and opens it, rummaging through buttons, zips and spools upon spools of utilitarian black, white and brown thread, before finally finding a pair of sharp scissors. They cut through the rope and the sack falls open to reveal a thick bolt of khaki cloth, the kind used to make utilitarian army and police uniforms. The material is of poor quality, hardly better than the burlap it came wrapped in, the fibres catching on Gul Khan's dry and cracked fingertips as he runs his hands over it.

Every five months or so, he gets the same package with the cardboard like cloth, a set of instructions and an envelope of brown and sea-blue rupees, worn and faded from being passed around countless hands. The Commander is nothing if not fair, thinks Gul Khan mockingly, paying him generously for his labour. There had been a time when he had refused to take the package, when he had considered himself brave, his principles and morals inflexible, vowing loudly to anyone who would listen that he would never work for the Commander. But that had been before the soldiers dragged him out of his house and tied him, naked, to the electric post outside the police station. Fifteen strokes of the lash and Gul Khan had been tamed.

The Commander's handwriting is small, the words squirming across the page like tiny black ants. Gul Khan brings the page closer to his face, frowning as he tries to decipher the order. He knows from experience that the measurements for the vests will be precise to the last millimetre, for the Commander requires them to sit snug against his recruits' chests, undetectable under clothes. He takes out his tape measure and spreads the cloth out on the floor, marking out the dimensions for the vests with a blue wax crayon. The first two are simple enough, but the last one, he realizes in confusion, is much too small. The Commander never makes mistakes, but even knowing that, Gul Khan re-measures the cloth, once, twice, thrice. It is only once the swipe of the crayon confirms the child sized dimensions, that he finally understands.

Gul Khan shuffles back from the cloth as if it hides a nest of vipers. He has become accustomed to the helpless guilt he feels each time he completes the Commander's orders, bearing it by wrapping himself in the sweet oblivion of opium. But this new vest threatens to destroy his desperately patched together peace. His nostrils flare, remembering the metallic, coppery scent of his blood as it splattered on the road and he knows that he needs to leave his house, to go somewhere where he can breathe freely. He stumbles into the narrow, muddy street, which, besides the occasional bleat of a goat is heavy with silence. It should have been echoing with the chatter of women on their way to the morning market, but it is as if a *jinn* has wiped them off the face of this earth. There is a sticky, viscous quality to this enforced muteness which clings to Gul Khan, making him feel like a fly trapped in jelly, sinking deeper and slowly suffocating.

Walking as quickly as he can, he crosses the market where young men in uniform sit at a café sipping tea, their Kalashnikovs held carefully on their laps like long lost lovers. He knows most of them, having measured them for clothes when they were smooth faced village boys and not the bearded, glowering men they had become. Sweat trickles down his turbaned head and the scars on his back flare to life as he nods to them, a quick, respectful bow acknowledging their dominance over him. They had shouted and watched, their faces contorted in glee like children at a football match, as the Commander stripped and tied him to the post.

His path leads him past the old school, now a *madrassah*. Through the open door, he sees rows upon rows of boys sitting on woven mats on the floor, learning only about the Commander's God and his ancient laws. Their voices thrum in the air, like a buzzing swarm of bees, as they sway over open copies of their holy book. Monitors carrying thick, heavy sticks patrol the rows, stopping now and then to strike a swaying boy. The sound of wood hitting flesh, a loud, wet thwack, makes Gul Khan flinch in sympathy as he scuttles away.

The road circles around fields of ruby red poppies bobbing in the breeze guarded by bored looking soldiers. Beyond the poppy fields, the road turns into a dirt track that winds up the mountain, used by shepherds and their charges, whose pebbly droppings litter the ground like tiny, black berries. The climb, though gentle, makes Gul Khan's legs tremble and his breath come in a sharp wheeze. It is the only sound for miles, except for the occasional, desolate "baa" followed by a shepherd's shrill whistle. But this silence is different. It is unburdened by the stain of their collective cowardice and collusion. It is the restful quiet of a warm spring afternoon when the sun's heat sinks through layers of skin and flesh to warm the bones and a gentle breeze brings with it the saccharine perfume of apple blossoms.

Gul Khan stops at the edge of the path to lean against an apple tree, its branches curving over his head to form a dome of dainty white and pink blossoms. The lacy filigree reminds him of the delicate scroll work painted on the ceiling of the old village mosque, the one the soldiers blew up to build their own plain, concrete one. He lowers himself to the ground with a groan, feeling slow and stiff, the valley spreading below his feet like a living tapestry, as if nature itself was rebelling against the grey and beige strictures of the Commander. Streams like shimmering, silver snakes wind and tumble into deceptively icy lakes. The distance reduces his village to a jumble of brown boxes, like the mud houses he used to make along the river banks as a child, surrounded by a shimmering sea of bloody flowers.

Cutting off a small twig of blossoms from the branch above him, Gul Khan places it behind his ear. "How can this not be enough?" he mutters to himself. "Why do they have to go looking for rivers of sweet milk and honey?" He takes out a pipe from his pocket and a small, rolled clump of opium that looks like a melted blob of chocolate. He looks around, shifting his body so that he is hidden from the path, as taking drugs is forbidden by the Commander and is punishable by death. The irony of this makes Gul Khan want to howl with laughter. He lights the pipe, takes a few puffs then lies down on the soft grass.

Through the branches the cloudless sky looks like an immense turquoise jewel, its surface marred by a single, white foamy line left behind by a tiny jet plane. He feels disoriented, unmoored, as if the world has upturned itself, that the sky is now a vast blue lake he could tumble into and drown.

His last thought, as his eyes close, is how easy it would be to fall into infinity.

It is evening by the time he makes his way back home. With the sapphire of the sky and the ruby red of the fields still fresh in his mind, he takes out a piece of paper and sketches rows upon rows of poppies, sprigs of apple blossoms and round apricots. He is gripped by an excitement that he thought he had lost as he flings open a battered suitcase full of hoarded scraps of vibrant, soft silks in chartreuse and magenta and orange. This is the sum of his years as a tailor, all that remains of the beautiful and heavily decorated clothes he used to make for weddings and festivals. From a jumble of embroidery threads, he chooses a deep red for the poppy petals with a dark, purple-black for the middle, pale pink and white for the apple blossoms and a shiny gold for the apricots. He picks a square of blue silk for the tapestry, smaller than his forearm, the exact colour of the sky, and spreads it on his wooden tailor's block. He begins to trace the design onto the cloth using the last of his carbon paper. Then, careful of smudging the ink, he stretches the cloth tight between two embroidery hoops.

His hands shake and it takes him several tries before his arthritic fingers finally manage to thread the needle. He works late into the night and then into the next few days, stooping over the hoop, lost once again to the magic and joy of creation. His fingers have forgotten the feel of the long embroidery needle, so that the first few stitches are rough and uneven as he starts to outline the fruit and flowers in his tapestry. Several times the needle slips and pricks his fingers, the drops of blood blossoming like wild flowers on the cloth, but soon enough his body remembers and his fingers fly, filling the cloth with tiny, dense stitches.

By the third day his fingers are cramping, his back aching from the hours bowed over the embroidery hoop, but he is finally finished. He looks around him in a daze for his work had transported him somewhere else, a place where beauty and colour and his talent with a needle mattered and wasn't just another skill to be exploited in the name of God. The tapestry is not his best, nor his neatest work. Some of the stitches are crooked and the fabric is frayed where he has pulled too hard on the thread, but it is a riot of colour, life seeping through the cloth in the shape of flowers and blossoms. It is, he knows, breathtaking.

He jumps as someone knocks on the door.

"Gul Khan! Gul Khan, are you home?

Recognising the voice of his friend Yousaf, the old man hides the tapestry under his bed and opens the door.

"Where have you been? I haven't seen you at the mosque for prayers in days, old man." Yousaf follows Gul Khan into the kitchen, sitting down on a low stool next to the gas stove.

Gul Khan shrugs, his mind still occupied with colours and threads, as he puts a kettle on for tea. "Here. Working."

"Well, be careful. You don't want the soldiers to notice and come sniffing around." Noticing how Gul Khan struggles to straighten up from the stove, Yousaf asks, gently, "Is your back hurting again?" He digs into his pocket and pulls out a small plastic bag. "Here. I waited for you at the mosque, but when you didn't show up I got worried and thought I'd check up on you."

Gul Khan takes the packet, turning it over in his hands. In the feverish trance of the past few days, he hadn't felt the desire to smoke, but now, the sudden force of the craving shakes him.

"It's all I could spare, so don't smoke it all in one go," warns Yousaf.

Gul Khan hands him a tin cup brimming with sweet tea before going into his room. He takes out the money from the Commander's envelope and counts out the payment for the opium.

Yousaf accepts the money with an embarrassed nod and quickly hides it in his pocket. He grows poppies for the Commander, skimming off the crop and selling opium to those desperate souls like Gul Khan searching for oblivion. It is a dangerously twisted, yet lucrative form of revenge against the Commander, one which, fears Gul Khan, will have his friend hanging from the nearest electric pole.

The two men sit sipping their tea in silence. Suddenly Yousaf puts his cup down and says, "Do you remember my sister's youngest son, the one with the gap in his front teeth?" He taps his own front teeth for emphasis as Gul Khan nods. He had seen the boy almost a year ago to measure him for a new tunic for Eid. Tall and unused to his new height, the boy had been unable to stand still, until finally losing all patience, Gul Khan had smacked him on the head.

"He didn't come home from *madrassah* a few weeks ago. When I went looking for him they said that he had volunteered to join the soldiers. Can you imagine? The boy is not even thirteen." Yousaf rubs his eyes and sighs. "What can they want with him? Every day my sister and I go to the station, begging to see the child, but they say that he doesn't want anything to do with us. My sister's heart is broken." He goes quiet then gives Gul Khan a quick, furtive glance. "I was wondering if you had heard anything?" he asks quietly.

Gul Khan puts his cup down slowly. There had been a small part of him which had hoped to never know the identity of the child soldier. He opens his mouth, but the words shrivel into dust in his mouth. How can Yousaf or his sister ever understand? And what good would it do to fill their heads with fears of things they can do nothing about. They will never get him back. The boy does not belong to them anymore.

He looks down and shakes his head.

"Forgive me for burdening you with this, you have enough worries of your own." Yousaf stands and lays a hand on Gul Khan's shoulder. "It's not a new story. So many men and boys lost. Allah have mercy!"

When Yousaf leaves, Gul Khan goes back to his room and lays the tapestry out on his bed, but instead of the rows of poppies, apple blossoms and frosty blue mountains, he sees the boy's gap-toothed smile. "What did they promise you?" he wonders aloud, his shaking fingers moving tenderly over the cloth, the silk now stiff with embroidery. "Did they hold a gun to your head or did you raise your hands and volunteer, visions of paradise dancing behind your eyes?"

That evening he finally starts stitching the vests. They are square, utilitarian garments with rows of deep pockets and small holes for the wires to run through, so different from the soft *kurtas* and *peshwas* he once made. He takes special care when it is time to sew the boy's vest, laying out the tapestry between the two panels of rough cloth with the gentleness of a mother putting a child to bed. Then, foot pumping up and down on the whirling treadle, he feeds the panels through his Singer until not a stitch of the tapestry is visible – a secret gift and prayer hidden inside the child's vest.

"May you think of home," Gul Khan whispers. He stitches a belt, then remembering the boy's skinny, gangly body, adds a few extra notches, just in case the vest is too big.

It takes him all night to finish the order. He folds the vests and places them back inside the burlap sack, using the last of his blue ribbons to tie it all together like a macabre gift. He leaves the parcel outside his door in the exact spot he had found it.

The early morning sun peeps from behind the smoky, blue mountains. Soon, he knows, its rays will strike the streams and turn them to liquid silver, passing over the valley to paint the poppy fields a brilliant red-gold, the colour of blood and fire. Gul Khan shivers in the crisp spring air, his body aching with a weariness that goes down to his bones.

"There is hope as long as there is beauty," he mutters to himself, though the words sound hollow and bleak. "Should be some comfort in that." He turns and slowly closes the door behind him.

Arif Anwar

Arif Anwar's debut novel, *The Storm*, was published internationally in 2018. His work has appeared in *Vice* magazine, *The Daily Star Bangladesh, Dhaka Tribune, The Daily Beast*, and *Electric Literature*, among others. He is currently hard at work on his second novel and a short story collection. He lives in Toronto, Canada.

Pig

I step out of the TTC and Mira trails me like a happy wraith and out come the first words she's said about being here (having come here second [after me] and having been sick for the first three months from pneumonia she caught on the plane that cost us three thousand dollars because she didn't have health insurance yet) and the words are about how cheap the things are at Honest Ed's and I tell her that it's still twice what it costs in Bangladesh and three times what it costs in China which is where all the stuff comes from anyway and she raises her eyebrows and says oh

Amin steps out of the TTC and i follow him the way i've been taught all my life that is not so close that we're equals even though it's unstated but not so far so that people think he's not mine and the only thing i can think of is how cheap things are in Canada because it wasn't something i'd ever dreamed possible that you could have safety security and economy all in the same place but here we are but he frowns and says that the prices at Honest Ed's aren't that impressive after all because it's all from China and it'd be half the price still back in Bangladesh and i just say oh because he came here before me and I think of the saying back home that our parents drilled into our (her) head(s) about a wife's heaven being under her husband's feet and the first time Mira's mother said it to her she told me she laughed but it died on her lips when her mother didn't join in but I had heard the same thought expressed in films and from others, sometimes ironically from my friends who married earlier than me and I put it out of my mind because it didn't really concern me and really why should I have to think about it because now five years have gone by in the blink of an eye in which I haven't had pig yet since coming here or even a drink even though I worked as a bartender that one summer at Mel's where I studied every single simple drink even memorizing the words in the cocktail recipe book but never tasted or even licked a finger that time I cleaned up a spilled amaretto sour and I was really

and i am the child here and he the parent but no more parents even though the ones i left back home who i still dutifully call almost every night using a phone card that makes me punch in oh so many numbers ask more after him and how he's doing than me as though Amin did us a big favour by marrying me by flipping through a catalog and then picking out my picture that he told the ghotok he liked and then the man made the arrangements between the two families but i can't comprehend how he could spend five years here five years through the frigid winter and the endless grey days and i wonder if he's ever taken a drink or if he's ever been tempted and what man wouldn't with all that he's surrounded with all these incredibly beautiful women wearing next to nothing and their swaying breasts in the summer hasn't he ever wanted or wondered or is that something we decide never to think about tempted but I couldn't and in the end that night I went home and prayed the tarabi which means extra rakats and getting up and doing washing myself in the middle of the night and that was always hard for me but I did it anyway and the next week I quit the job to cut myself off from the temptation, but pig, no.

We walk and walk and walk in the heat and the temp reader pasted to the side of the building says it's 37 in BIG RED NUMBERS and the humidity is close to Dhaka's and Mira says she doesn't mind and even likes it for it reminds her of home for it's going to rain later when the first drops will hit the ground to give off that smell that I love and she loves too but I don't know that yet that two people can share a love of the indescribable scent of home.

I nod and tell her that I'm glad that the heat is tolerable and familiar but what I don't say

cause it's forbidden to us like the fruit that Adam and Eve weren't allowed to eat but ended up eating anyway and that's just the way it is isn't it when you're walking by the muck everyday some'll spatter on your clothes.

That's inevitable.

It's hot so hot so wonderfully hot and it's like i've been given life for the first time since coming to this country and for the first time it feels like home with this muggy heat pressing down on me like a fat old friend.

We pass a Swiss Chalet and i've always wanted to eat there because it's on the tv all the time but i haven't had the courage to try any fast food so far in these months i've been in Canada not McDonalds not KFC not Burger King not Taco bell not not not not not Wendys (?) all those legendary names (not a single one Canadian) i heard of as a child but now within a walk's reach but i never went in once because i didn't think is that we're saving six dollars by walking from Bathurst to Jane (crime crime crime crime) to our efficiency where she'll cut up and cook the fish and vegetables we've bought from Taj Mahal Foods (make rice) and it's been so long that I've had fish that wasn't cooked (badly) by someone other than me, but my stomach's growling and I'm sure that hers is too but she's still cheerful and uncomplaining until we finally pass a Swiss Chalet I ask her if she wants to try it and when she says yes I'm both happy and worried because that's fifteen dollars we don't really have but that doesn't really concern her and really why should it?

We go in and look at the menu above the heavy girl in the too-tight polo and when I ask Mira what looks good to her she says the ribs so that's what we order and secretly I loosen a little bit because it's on special and just 4.95 a combo says polo-girl all the while eyeing Mira's hijab

Amin would like it because he wants to stay here and insulate himself as though Canada is just a coat he puts on to go outside and takes off once he gets home so i point at the Swiss Chalet and ask him if he wants to go there and try it and he pretends not to hear me and then asks if i want to try Swiss Chalet because home is still a half hour's walk away and i say 'yes' and he looks slightly annoyed.

We go in and look at the menu and at the counter below is a girl with the body i always wanted because i was skin and bones when i came here and now i'm that even more (three day hospital stay and three thousand dollars) and the girl is young and has pimples but there's a sweetness to her face and she's staring at me and at my hijab so i hide behind Amin because I can't take this scrutiny and I'm still not used to it.

I see it enough on the street.

Amin points at the ribs and

which makes her hide behind me because she's still shy about her English but soon the food arrives and we start to eat and it doesn't taste right not even close – too sweet too tender the small bones oh God but Mira next to me is happily chewing away a small dab of the red sauce at the corner of her mouth. She has no idea and the girl at the counter is staring at us with big eyes as if some belated realization has come over her that she should have said or asked... something. So maybe there was credit to give her after all but in the end she didn't say anything did she?

I look around to see if someone we know is here.

Can I say anything? Can I say anything about what we're eating that won't have Mira make a scene by crying or retching in public? There isn't.

She's cleaned out half the pieces already and is sucking on a tiny bone and that makes my stomach flip but I stop myself

asks me if that looks good and i know that he's eyeing it because it's on special just 4.95 per combo but oh god does he not know how can he not know so i say 'yes' just to see how he reacts and if he'll order it and he does because he really doesn't know.

It arrives and we eat and it's not as hard as i thought it would be to put the first piece in my mouth and chew and the flesh is more tender than beef but also more flavourful and all this time i thought that when and if this moment came i'd probably throw up and wouldn't be able to do it but i am and i can and i am all the while Amin next to me is slowing down as he realizes what it is even though he's never had it before.

He asks me if i like it and i say yes and pretend to not know and he's now looking around as though someone we might know might see what we're eating and come and shame us.

He asks me to stop.

somehow by looking outside the window and somehow keeping it all down with force of will. Ribs. It just said ribs. It didn't say beef ribs. Stupid. Stupid stupid.

My eating meanders to a stop. Mira's on her second stack. I tell her that I'm done and that she ought to save room for dinner.

Why?

Because I've stopped eating so I thought you might want to save some room as well too.

Why?

I'll cook tonight. I want it to be special.

She does but looks resentful. Your mother told me you can't cook.

I will tonight, for you. Stop eating. Please.

She tells me sullenly that she wants to pack it for home.

That's fine, I think. I'll throw it away when she's not looking cause I can't ever tell her. I can't. No good can come of it. I can shrug off the taint, but she can't.

I ask him why.

He says because he'll cook tonight and he doesn't want me to fill up too much and i just say 'you don't cook' and he says that he will.

I tell him that i want to pack it for home.

I don't even know if i mean it but i feel exhilarated and alive all the while Amin thinks he's trying to save me and that he's going to save me.

We step out and beautiful curvy pimple girl is staring at us both and i give her a smile and Amin is in front of me again and we're walking out again into the glorious sunshine and once in the heat of the day again is when i feel nauseous and proud.

Now it's time to go home for my love where i'll cut and clean and cook the fish for him with my loving hands and he'll love me for i've made him a hero and he'll bear this knowledge in silence shame and pride and for the years that we have together

I've to bear it for the both us.

We rise to leave and the plastic container of leftovers swings too heavily in my hand. The polo girl is staring at us wide-eyed.

Three years. Three years from now we'll fight and she'll spit at me and say I never loved her not once and when that happens I'll remember. I won't say it but I'll remember and smile and say to myself 'I did'.

the years that we will have together it'll be the secret that he doesn't know we both hold and that holds us fast together for that's what secrets are.

Glue.

Erika Banerji

Erika Banerji was born in Assam, India, and educated in New Delhi and London. Her short stories have been published in journals and listed for awards including the Lorian Hemingway, V. S Pritchett and London Short Story Prize. She was longlisted for The Bath Novel Award in 2016. In 2019 her short story was in the top sixty entries in The BBC National Short Story Award. She is an alumni of the Faber Academy 'Writing a Novel' Course and the London Library Emerging Writers Program 2019-20. Erika lives in London and is currently working on a novel and a collection of stories. www.erikabanerji.com Twitter @erikabanerji

Marvellous Real

There were guests expected at the apartment on Kabir Road, but it would not be until evening. Gopal knew he was by himself for the next three hours whilst the Mitra family were at the Tolly Club. So, he sat with his feet up on the green velvet couch in the living room and thought about how he might use his time alone.

The washing up and dusting could wait.

He went straight into the children's room at the back of the flat and climbed to the top bunk and lay down and watched the slow whirl of the ceiling fan above him. His own bedding, which comprised a thin mattress and a faded sheet, were in one of the kitchen cupboards. At night he laid it on the kitchen floor.

The pillow on the bunk felt uncomfortable, and he rubbed his neck and ran his finger along the outline of the funny shaped green animals on the covers.

'*Dinosaur*,' he'd heard the children call them. He wondered where creatures like this lived.

Gopal climbed down and went into the bathroom. Standing on tiptoes, he stared at himself in the mirror.

He brushed his teeth with the blue brush with a picture of a turtle man on it and ate an extra squeeze of toothpaste he took onto his forefinger. He wet his hair and combed it flat with the hairbrush. The mirror was cloudy, speckled with age.

He stuck out his tongue.

In the bedroom he opened doors and peered into cupboards. He went through the contents of a drawer. He uncorked a bottle of rosewater and its fragrance escaped to mingle with the talcum powder he patted liberally on his chest. Then he went to the toy chest that stood at the end of the bed. He stared at it for a while. The afternoon sun angled through the window shutters, bouncing off the metal hinges which he shone each day to a high polish.

The lid was heavy. Inside, the Man-doll lay right at the top of the pile of toys. Underneath he spotted a cricket ball and miniature bat, a twisted skipping rope and several tiny cars and buses and trucks with missing wheels. There was a bag of colourful plastic building bricks. Last week Gopal had found a yellow brick under the bed when he was sweeping the room. He'd put it in his pocket and taken it up to his secret stash-tin behind the water tank on the roof.

He'd waited a long time to hold the Man-doll in his hands. It was lighter than he'd imagined. He stroked the cold ripples of the chest muscles and the taut stomach. He lifted his shirt and checked the soft roundness of his own belly. He sucked in his breath to see if he could make his stomach taut. He stroked the head of the doll, the light fuzz of its tight crewcut, then stared at the sharp blue eyes. He'd never seen eyes that colour. Everyone in his family, his parents and two brothers, had dark brown eyes. Except on those nights when his father drank the muddy liquid out of the newspaper-wrapped bottle.

Then his father's eyes were blazing red.

Gopal was glad he only got to see his father once a month when he came to collect his son's salary from Mrs Mitra, or Madam, as he'd been instructed to call her.

He slipped the doll into the pocket of his shorts and made his way out of the flat, through the back door and up the servant's staircase, making sure he put the door on the latch. The door to the flat above opened, and Mina the maid appeared.

'Where are you off to?' she asked. Her sari was wet at the hem, as if she'd been wading through water.

'To the roof,' Gopal said.

'What you got in your hand?'

'Nothing,' he said. Mina didn't like him because she'd wanted her nephew to get his job, but her nephew was just six, and that was far too young for the Mitra's so they'd chosen Gopal who was nearly eight. Mina resented that her family had missed out on an extra income because of Gopal.

'Make sure you stay away from my laundry,' she said and glared at him.

Gopal flattened himself against the wall, holding the doll behind his back.

Up on the roof, which was on the fifth floor of the apartment-block, Gopal sat in the shade of the water tank. He took out the small tin he kept hidden behind the pipes. It was an old discarded biscuit tin. On the lid was a faded picture of a child eating an enormous biscuit. Inside was the yellow plastic brick, a broken pencil, two buttons which had fallen off the boy's school shirts and a rusty blade. He put the tin aside and stared at the doll, wished he could be as still and cool as him. It was barely three in the afternoon and not a single cloud lingered on the horizon. A clothesline ran from a hook on the tank wall to a bamboo pole erected in the corner. A red and yellow printed sari whipped back and forth in a steady hot wind that blew from the south.

Gopal lifted the Man-doll's arms one at a time, swivelled them around in an expansive gesture. The doll wore khaki trousers and a vest. Its arms bulged with strength. Around its waist was a thin plastic belt with a tiny metal buckle. Gopal lay on his belly on the coarse hot cement and walked the doll up and down before him. He undressed it, carefully unbuckling the belt, slipping off the vest. Then he smoothed his fingers over the contours of its limbs, the hinges at its hips, the ambiguity between its legs. He dressed it again and sat it down with its legs wide apart to eat an imaginary meal.

'Please have a plate of Biryani, Man-doll,' Gopal said and he made loud smacking sounds with his mouth to pretend the doll was eating. 'Would you care for more *mishti*?' he said and held an imaginary plate delicately in his hands as Mrs Mitra had taught him when he was to offer guests. 'They are *Bancharam's* best *Lebu-Shandesh*,' he said.

He shared with the Man-doll all the things he loved to eat but rarely ever tasted. When the family downstairs had guests, he often got the leftovers after he'd cleaned up and washed the dishes. Sometimes the leftovers were put away in the fridge. Often forgotten and thrown in the bin a week later.

Once, as Gopal collected the dishes from the table after the family had finished dinner, he saw a piece of mutton left on the younger son's plate. Back in the kitchen, he slipped it into his mouth as he stacked the dishes into the sink. Just then Mrs Mitra came into the kitchen. She gave him a resounding smack on the back of his head.

'That's stealing,' she said to him, 'it wasn't offered to you.' She made him spit it out into the bin.

'Eat as much as you can,' Gopal said to the Man-doll. After the feast, he licked his lips and smacked his own tummy, ignoring the hollow gurgle from within. Lunch had been a while ago. Then, he tucked the Man-doll into the crook of his arm and lay back, staring up at the cloudless sky.

It was almost five o'clock when Gopal startled awake.

'Hey, lazy boy,' said Mina. She was collecting the washing, which was now brittle from the sun. 'I saw the Mitra's car pull into the parking lot downstairs,' She hummed a tune as she threw the pegs into a plastic container.

He scrambled to his feet, forgetting for a moment that the doll lay beside him, and then he heard a crunch and a sharp stab at his left foot. Looking down, he saw he'd stepped on the doll. Its right arm snapped off and lay awkwardly beside it. He picked up the doll and its dismembered arm and as he raced back downstairs, his head pounded and his lips were dry.

'What happened to my Action Man?' said Sandip, the Mitra's eldest son, to his mother. 'It's broken.'

'What do you mean broken, it was fine when you played with it last, wasn't it?'

His mother was putting a garnish of coriander on a plate of mutton patties, spreading the green leaves in a delicate flourish.

Gopal squatted on the floor underneath the sink, scouring the blackened insides of a wok. He'd been told-off for neglecting the afternoon's dishes. His back smarted from the slap. But he thought he'd got off lightly. He was more worried about the broken doll which he'd hurriedly pushed into the toy box.

'Go ask your brother if he knows anything,' Mrs Mitra said, busy arranging the plates and forks on a tray. She tucked triangles of paper napkins between each plate.

Sandip went away to find his brother.

'The guests will be here any minute,' she said, 'make sure you bring this plate in after the teapot.'

'Yes, Madam,' Gopal said. The pan gleamed with the extra effort he put into the scrubbing. He must have more muscle power like the Man-doll, he thought and smiled to himself. He wondered who the guests would be.

The doorbell rang and Gopal peered through the serving hatch.

Mr and Mrs Basu from the flat above handed a box of sweets to Sandip and his brother Sujoy.

'We hear you both have been good boys,' Mr Basu, a short middle-aged man with a bristly moustache said winking at them. The boys took the box and giggled and ran off without waiting to say thank you. Mrs Mitra ushered the couple into the living room, which opened onto the front balcony. Outside the evening unfurled on Kabir Road with the ring of passing rickshaws and the beeping of car horns. A conch shell blew at the local temple.

Gopal busied himself with the tea things. He boiled the water in the large aluminium kettle, then poured it carefully into the china teapot. Mrs Mitra had already measured out the tea leaves. A bit of water splattered onto his hands, but he didn't flinch. He placed the teapot carefully on the tray, counted out the cups.

On his way to the living room he passed the boys sitting in front of the television in their parent's bedroom. A duck waddled on the colourful screen. It wore a sweater and sat at a table to eat. Gopal paused outside their door. They never invited him to join them. Once he'd asked Sandip where such ducks lived and the boys had burst out laughing. Since then they quacked like a duck at him whenever they needed someone to annoy.

Gopal didn't really mind.

The box of sweets was open and discarded on the floor beside them. Gopal wondered if they were the soft brown *natun gur* ones popular at this time of year.

The tray was wide and heavy and his arms ached by the time he got to the living room. He hoped he wouldn't have to hold on to it for too long. He stood at the door until Mrs Mitra gestured to him to come forward.

He placed the tray carefully on the coffee table. His arms felt longer, strained from the shoulder sockets.

'Is this your new houseboy,' Mrs Basu said. She was a thin woman with a face, that Gopal thought, looked a bit like a goat. Thick gold bangles jangled each time she moved. Mrs Basu's eyes were on him as he placed each cup on a saucer, then handed it to Mrs Mitra to pour the tea.

'Yes, his family live underneath Tolly Bridge, you know, in that decrepit slum that keeps growing there.' Mrs Mitra said without even looking towards him. 'They were glad to have him grafted.'

'The Tollygunge Municipality should really do something about them,' Mrs Basu said, 'it's becoming quite an eyesore every time we need to get to the Tolly Club.'

Gopal handed around the teacups. He held the saucers with both hands to make sure nothing would spill.

'Sometimes it's hard really, training them,' Mrs Mitra said, 'he knew nothing when he started.'

He went to the kitchen and brought back the carefully arranged platter of mutton patties.

Mrs Mitra watched him like a hawk as he walked around the room with the platter. Sometimes Gopal believed that she hoped he'd make a mistake just so she could tell him off.

He needed the toilet, but he could hold it for a bit.

Mr Basu picked a mutton patty off the plate Gopal held before him. His heavy jowls drooped over the starched collar of his shirt.

'What was Mina telling you earlier this evening?' he said to his wife. Gopal became conscious of the sound of his own breathing, the pressure in his bladder.

'Your boy was up on the roof most of the afternoon it seems,' Mrs Basu said. Her husband smacked his lips and reached for another patty.

'Yes, the rooftop holds many delights for the boy. Not sure what, though,' Mrs Mitra said. She nodded to him to put the platter down on the table.

He felt as if he was drowning.

'Did you say his father is a drunk?'

'Aren't they all?' Mrs Mitra sighed, 'either drunks or gamblers who beat their wives and send their kids to work. And we have to be socially obliged to use them,'

Above them, the fan squeaked. Gopal hoped that it might fall on top of him, smash him.

He handed out some extra napkins.

'Mina said he had a doll with him,' There was a determined jut to Mrs Basu's chin as she spoke. She took the napkin from Gopal and looked at the green and pink floral pattern with interest. She patted her mouth and then resumed eating.

Gopal opened the back door and stood in the stairwell's darkness alone. His bare feet were cold against the mosaic floor. A breeze that came through the slatted cement sides lifted the hair off his forehead. Goosebumps covered his arms.

He held the one-armed Man-doll against his chest and slipped up the stairs in the dark.

Up on the rooftop, the moon was lifeless. Just a blemish against the dark night. Below, on Kabir road, a few of the streetlights no longer worked. A dog howled as it stood alone next to a heap of discarded rubbish.

Gopal felt the bruise on his left shoulder where Mrs Mitra had whacked him with a broom. She'd picked a spiky broom, made of thin reeds used to sweep water off the bathroom floors.

It had ripped his shirt all across his shoulders, leaving a zig zag of blood and peeling skin.

'I shall take the price of the toy out of your salary,' she said and held him by the scruff of his neck and pushed his face into the wall. He'd felt the searing pain of the wall as it hit his face, the heat of the blood that dripped out of his nose onto his shirt, the quacking of a duck.

A passing car sent its liquid glare into the leaves of the Shimul trees on the opposite side of the road. Above, in the starless sky, were the flashes of planes flying to places he'd only dreamt of and made him long for a different world.

Gopal climbed onto the low wall of the roof and looked at the surrounding neighbourhood, the tangle of wires rising out of the electricity poles and the rain-tarnished walls of apartment blocks around him. Below, the night watchman blew his whistle and went past dragging his stick.

He thought of ducks wearing sweaters and sitting in chairs, of the one-armed Man-doll, of Biryani and soft white *Sandesh* from *Bancharam*. He thought of his father's red eyes when he'd collect his salary this month.

'Let's fly Man-doll,' he whispered to the doll he'd tucked into the front of his shirt.

He spread his arms wide and jumped.

Ethan Chapman

Ethan Chapman's short fiction has been published in *Popshot* magazine, *Structo* magazine, by Otherwhere Publishing, as well as been shortlisted for the Frome Short Story Competition. His poetry has been published in *Agenda* and *Firewords Quarterly*. He is currently working on his first novel.

Where Have All the Children Gone?

I n the days that follow there will be things to do. There will be statements to the police and statements to the media. There will be numbers set up for leads and information. There will be search parties organised and posters made with her daughter's face on them. The posters will fill her house and they will fill the streets. They will be posted on bulletin boards and walls and telephone poles. They will be placed under the wipers of cars and pushed through letterboxes and they will be placed in shop and living room windows.

So that in the days after her disappearance her daughter will not be gone completely. Her face will be everywhere, as if watching them all, observing. She will linger in every thought, every conversation. She will be both gone and not gone; here and not here. Both everywhere and nowhere.

Her house will fill with people – police officers, volunteers, strangers. Her life will become chaotic and loud and full of moving parts. They will set up action stations in her kitchen. They will look at maps and plot over them as if they are planning to invade a country. They will take calls from a phone that will ring continuously and they will glance at her while they talk to each other in code. They will surround her, trip over her. They will make her tasteless cups of tea and try to comfort her in cool, matter of fact voices. They will tell her they are doing everything that can be done, and she will nod and know it isn't close to being enough; there will always be something else they should be doing, something else that could be done. Her daughter will still be out there somewhere and, with every second that passes, she will feel the two of them being pulled further apart; feel her being buried deeper inside the world, every passing moment making her more lost.

She will be led into a gym hall and seated at a table overlooking people armed with cameras and questions. She will feel like a circus animal being stared at. Her mother will sit on one side of her. She will hold her hand and whisper that everything will be okay, and she will struggle to feel her, struggle to hear her. On the other side of her will sit the police officer heading the investigation. He will tell the people everything they need to know and everything the public needs to know, which will be close to nothing. The information will be the same as always – a missing child, last seen somewhere near her home, a call for witnesses.

She will also have to speak. She will have to say things into the camera, things like "Wherever you are, please just let us know you're okay" and "Please come back to us" and "I love you" and her voice will seem strange to her, distant. The words will seem lifeless, lacking the things most needed to translate, to get to where her daughter can find them.

She will rarely be able to sleep. It will feel like giving over responsibility. It will feel like giving up.

Instead she will relive the evening her daughter disappeared. She will remember looking out the living room window and waiting for her to come home. She will remember the seconds inching past. She will remember glancing up the path, the faint hint of worry. Getting the dinner ready to distract herself, coming back and finding the path still empty. The look up to the sky. A thought: where is she? The darkening of the evening and the worry spreading along with the dark. The rationalising, the messing with her hands, the looking at the clock, the anger. Another thought: damn it, where is she? The pacing until the eventual giving in to worry. The frantic calling of numbers, people telling her they haven't seen her. The panic, the rush outside. The overwhelming feeling that the world is just too wide, just much too large for one little girl. The knocking on doors. The people out looking. The evening now dark. The people coming back shaking their heads. Trying to rationalise with herself. Failing. Being led back home and sitting down in the darkness, the emptiness. People sat by her. The police being called. The panic slowly giving way to understanding that something is wrong. That what she has feared has finally come to pass.

Though her daughter going missing is a terrible thing, she will wonder if it's the worst thing. What's worse may be the reminders – the pictures of her daughter on the walls, the school bag under the stairs, the school shoes left by the door, the sharp tightening of her stomach when she sees them.

What's worse may be the sympathetic friends and neighbours who will bludgeon her with their compassion. They will be the voices on the phone, the knocks on the door, the calls through the windows, the intruders in her life. They will stop her in the street and say how sorry they are and tell her if there's anything they can do. They will put their hands on their own children when they speak to her and grasp them tight. They will stop talking when they see her walk into the supermarket, into the bank. They will speak about her daughter in the past tense when she's gone.

She will know that when these children are taken it's nearly always someone the child knows, and she will treat her whole life with suspicion. She will place it under the microscope, try to remember anyone strange her daughter might have mentioned. She will make a list of suspects and no one will be off limits. She will suspect her friends, her family, everyone. She will blame them all. She will blame the people in her house for not finding her and she will blame her own mother for giving birth to her. She will blame the culture and the world and the men that roam above it all. She will blame her daughter for not coming back to her. She will blame herself for thinking she could ever keep her daughter safe.

She will visit her daughter's room. The atmosphere will be different now; will feel like a separate world, one independent of the one she normally occupies. She will run her hands along the wall, along the edges of her unmade bed, over the pictures of her daughter's friends. She will run her hands over the pictures of her daughter herself and be able to feel the faint outlines of her face, her skin. She will be able to feel her daughter's presence still occupying this room, her leftover energy, and she will feel an absence in her heart and in her soul that's clearer and closer than anything she has ever experienced. Her world will start to tilt and she will have to flee the room. She will shut the door, lean hard against it, and hope that she hasn't allowed too much of her daughter's essence to escape. That she has trapped enough of it to stay.

There will be sightings and there will be leads and there will be dead ends. She will try not to lose hope. She will try not to hope too much.

They will spot her daughter in a shop in the next county over. They will see her getting in the back of a black van with an unidentified man. They will spot her getting on a bus with a strange woman.

The longer it goes on the further her daughter will get from her. They will spot her getting on planes and they will catch sight of her in different countries, staring down at them from hotel windows. She will hear the way people talk about it and read the way it is written. There will be a curiosity now – an interest, an excitement. There will be theories and there will be chat rooms and they will love the uncertainty of it all. She will feel her daughter ceasing to be hers and instead becoming theirs, some mystery that the world will enjoy thinking over, that they secretly hope is never solved.

The police will show her grainy photos of a girl walking in a field, sat watching television in a living room, looking out of the window of a car. They will all be different girls and yet they will all look just like her little girl. She will look closely – past the different hair, past the clothes that aren't hers – and see her daughter beneath it all. She will want every one of them to be her daughter so badly that she will think about saying yes, it's her. She will think about bringing one of these girls home as a replacement. Moulding her into her new daughter, just to cover over the cracks growing wider and deeper inside her. Then she will be disgusted with herself and she will shake her head, have to say no, and she will wonder how many times she will be made to go through this – the anticipation, the hope, the despair. She will see her life continuing this way – forever teetering on the precipice of salvation and oblivion.

She will know that from now on she will provide a service to the other parents. She will be the one it happened to, their worst fear. She will be a warning to them, a lesson. They will tell themselves they will not let what happened to her child happen to theirs. They will protect them. She will make them hold their children a little tighter, talk to them a little longer, love them a little harder. Before they go to sleep they will check the windows again, make sure the doors are locked again. They will kiss their children goodnight and then, after the children have fallen asleep, they will continue to watch them. They will think of her and her missing daughter, first with sadness and then, even though they'll never admit it, with relief. Thankful for the safety of their own children. Thankful it happened to her and not them.

One evening through the living room window she will watch her front garden ignite. Floating lights will bounce in the darkness and she will stand in the doorway with her mother and see a crowd gathered on her lawn. She will recognise her daughter's friends and children she has never seen. They will stand with lighted candles and their parents will stand close behind them. They will place a picture they've blown up and framed of her daughter's face – her last school photo, smiling her beautiful smile – at the base of a tree that her daughter would climb when she was young. She will watch them put down flowers and candles. They will stand and hold each other. It will be kind and thoughtful and overwhelming and exhausting. She will smile and say thanks. She will want them all to disappear. One of the friends, a girl whose name will escape her, will break off from the group and come toward her. She will look like she has something to say and will seem unsure of how to begin, and then someone will call her name, and the girl will say "I'm sorry" and turn away.

She will grow angry at the world. She will feel like she is not the kind of person this should happen to; that this should not be reserved for her.

She had always been careful with her daughter – ever since she was born, she'd been wary of the world. There were just so many places to get lost in, so much potential for chaos hidden in every second. She will remember her own mother telling her once that she herself had always felt like something was after her – was after *all* the children of the world – and it was up to the parents to keep the wolf from the door. She had been unsure but then she had had her own daughter and it was there; that maternal fear, running deep and true.

As her daughter got older, she would often feel that wolf getting closer and she would have to be more than careful. She would forbid her daughter from going to sleepovers, to discos, to parties, everything. She wouldn't want her out of her sight. Then years went by and she understood she'd have to let her live, but when she was gone she would feel the world hanging precariously, would feel that wolf getting closer, so she began to bargain with the world. She would touch things a number of times, whisper phrases that held the charge of good luck, walk over the same spot a number of times. She became certain there was some underlying current to the world, some cosmic deity she had to appease to keep her daughter safe. Sometimes she would wonder if she was losing her mind, but every day her daughter would still be there, safe, so she could never discount it completely. She just didn't want to be like the parents she saw on television. These people who had somehow misplaced their children and were now begging the public for help, for information, to be saved. They would always look the same – shocked, devastated, unprepared – as if it was the last thing they were expecting.

But now she will see that somewhere along the way the world

stopped listening. She will feel that the world hasn't kept up its end of the bargain, and she will feel not just the loss of her daughter but something else; a sense that the world has betrayed her.

She will do more interviews and beg the public to not lose interest, but soon the circus will die down and the world will begin to move on. The search parties will disperse and the people will go back to their own lives. She will watch her daughter's name slowly make its way toward the back of the newspapers until one day she is not there – replaced by another girl, another family. The people who have occupied her house for most of the summer will leave. Less and less mourners will come to her daughter's vigil until one day there are none. Her mother will go back to her own life. Before she goes, she will say that none of this is her fault, but for the first time she will see judgement in her mother's eyes, as if she has somehow failed some fundamental maternal test.

It will be just her left in her own house with the silence and the waiting. Her life will be given back to her and it will feel like an unwanted gift, a shape she can't fit herself into anymore. Her house will feel too wide and every room will feel familiar yet unrecognisable.

She will be unsure what is expected of her now, what she is to do. She will wonder how many more years she will have to keep doing this; how many more years she will have to wake up and feel those first few seconds of freedom, before her life clicks firmly back into place and she is reminded of what she has lost.

She will see the life ahead of her as a minefield she will have to navigate, full of things she will have to get through – birthdays, Christmases, the anniversary of her daughter's disappearance. Her life nothing but a waiting game, not just waiting for news of her daughter but waiting for the agony to ebb until it becomes a throbbing ache, something almost bearable. She will see the days balanced precariously in front of her, fragile and liable to spill. She will see herself growing old before her time, trying to keep the world at arm's length, desperately fighting to keep her head above water. But she will never outrun it. She will always be reminded – by a photo, by something. Her life forever changed and forever defined not by what is, but what isn't; by what doesn't inhabit it anymore.

Then one morning she will find her daughter standing on the porch. She will feel everything inside her contracting and condensing to a point, realigning, and then she will see it is not her daughter but some other girl. She will look familiar and it will take a while to place her, until she will recognise her as the girl from the vigil. She will feel everything holding her together grow slack and she will have to sit down. From somewhere above her the girl will ask if she can get her a drink, and she will say yes.

The girl will keep coming back. Day after day she will be stood at the door, waiting. She will help with the cleaning, with the washing, with everything she has neglected. She will see how messy she has allowed it to become and wonder how it got this bad. She will want nothing more than to be left alone, but slowly she will look forward to her coming around. She will look at her and find it easy to imagine that her daughter never left. She will look at the photos on the wall and the girl in front of her and sometimes be unable to tell the difference between them. She will imagine the days and weeks and months going by and substituting her daughter with this girl. She will imagine replacing the photos of her daughter with this girl. She will imagine layering over her daughter, replacing her entirely. It will all seem so plausible, so natural, and it will frighten her how easy it would be to bury herself inside this reality.

While out for a walk one afternoon, they will find one of her daughter's missing posters scrunched up and tossed behind an abandoned building. She will pick it up and smooth it out and look at the creased lines across her daughter's face, the yellowing colour of the paper. There will be smears of something red across it where it has been used to wipe something and she will hear the other girl start to cry. She will feel the frayed binds holding her together begin to tear. The world will turn cold and indifferent and she will not say a word. She will fold it up and put it in a spare carrier bag and they will spend the rest of the day going over town, picking up as many as they can find. They will go into shops and knock on houses and ask if they have pictures of her daughter. They will ignore the looks they receive. When they get home they will have two bags worth and she will put them in a corner of the living room. They will smell foul – a mixture of mildew and urine – but she will feel like she has reclaimed some vital part of her daughter that had been left out in the cold.

*

For days the posters will sit there and she will wonder what to do with them. The smell of urine will begin to fill the room. She will watch the girl cover her nose and mouth as she passes. When they sit down and watch television together they will try not to gag.

Sometimes she will catch her daughter's creased face staring back at her and she will wonder if she is in fact hurting her. That her daughter's disappearance wasn't something that happened to her but was perhaps a choice. That perhaps her daughter had wanted to escape from this world, and that by keeping these posters here she is somehow keeping some vital part of her daughter prisoner, a part that needs to be set free.

One morning she will not be able to take it anymore. She and the girl will dig a hole in the back garden and start a fire. They will watch it grow until they feel the heat resting on their faces. She will go in and grab the bag full of posters and bring them back out. The girl will watch her. She will reach in and grab a handful of them. The posters will feel sticky and rough and will irritate her hands. She will hesitate and then she will toss them in to the fire. She will watch the flames squeeze her daughter's face into blackness. It will hurt, will feel unbearable to watch her beautiful face warped by fire, but then she will feel something start to shift inside of her, something heavy that has been smothering her heart. She will feel it making room.

She will walk go back into the house and, after hesitating a moment, she will take the pictures of her daughter from the walls. She will come back out and throw them in the fire. She will feel that space getting wider. She will get her daughter's school bag, her shoes, and she will drag down her bedcovers. She will feel light and in flight and not in control. The girl will say nothing. She will go up into the attic and bring down the boxes of old schoolbooks, pictures of stick figures, paintings that say "I love you Mummy". She will burn them all, every one of her daughter's possessions. She will think about burning down her house and have to clench her fists to stop herself. She will feel the flames moulding and reshaping everything. She will feel everything tying her daughter to this world setting her free. It will feel cathartic and final, like her last act of being a mother.

They will watch the fire burn itself down to a flickering flame and she will look up and it will be evening. She will watch the shadows stretch in the golden twilight. She will think of the girl's mother waiting for her at home and she will tell her to get her coat.

On the way they will pass abandoned bikes and skipping ropes lying in bundles. They will not see one child and she will wonder where all the children have gone. She will whisper her daughter's name and already it will feel unfamiliar; a strange shape, something foreign on her tongue. She will try to recall her face and it will seem strange to her now, vague, like the blurred face of someone else's child. She will try to recall her voice and it will feel just out of reach, getting further away. Everything about her daughter diminishing, soon to be forgotten entirely.

They will get to the girl's house and the girl will manage a small smile and walk toward her front door. They will not say a word. She will watch her go inside and appear again in the living room where her mother has been waiting for her. She will see her mother smile with relief and embrace her. She will understand that this is a scene unavailable to her now, from a world she is leaving. A world where parents wait for their children to come home, where every day their lives are a second away from disaster, and she will feel relief and wonder how any of them survive childhood at all.

But just for a moment, before she turns away and leaves her old life forever, she will envy them. She will envy their love and their safety and their contact. She will envy their stupidity, their bravery. She will envy them all – every parent, every child. Every one of them who have never had to be found, because they have never been lost.

Chelsea Chong

Chelsea Chong is an emerging writer, based in Queensland, Australia. She spends her days frantically trying to capture the ideas floating around her mind before her one-year-old daughter insists on another reading of *The Very Hungry Caterpillar*. Inspired by the likes of C. S. Lewis and Anis Mojgani, Chelsea writes about the individual and collective search for identity with a focus on spirituality. She works as a freelance grant writer, holds a Masters in International Development, and has previously been a community development manager and English as an Additional Language teacher. She lives with her husband, Ben, and their young daughter, Hallie.

This is Not a Drill

'Trust me,' The Leader said. 'It is a new way. It is a better way. You will be safer and happier in the other place.' I hand over a bucket. I receive a bucket. Our skinny arms perform poorly. So many of them between us but hardly any water left when each bucket arrives. We pour dregs over wilting leaves and bitter fruit, fingers closing numb around the handles. Our compound is a circle cut in the centre of a jungle. The black cougars that stalk the perimeter are the only ones to come and go. They return time after time, patiently waiting, brushing silky fur along worn metal fences. We are easy prey. I sweep up wandering tendrils of dark thought and squash them into the bucket. Take it and hand it along. Take it and hand it along.

'I don't know if I can keep going.' My neighbour pushes through the humidity.

I look at the men and women, eyes bulging, sharp wrists knocking against bone and plastic and sultry air. I guess, like me, they thought more about the hunger in their souls before coming here. Now we stand side by side, a chain of bent and wiry figures, listening to our stomachs mock the people we used to be.

There is a hole in the dull hemp of my neighbour's shirt that stretches from her armpit to her hip. Through it I can see a hot red patch eating her flesh. The parting of her hair, sunburnt and flaking, disappears as she looks up at me.

'I'm too hungry,' she says.

I bark at her tired face, loud enough to be heard down the line. 'Get behind me with your wickedness. It's a better way.' *Head back down. Put your head back down Jane.* When I pass her the next bucket, I touch her hand in case she's not one of the spies The Leader has planted. Her eyes stay fixed on a crack of earth that runs under our feet and The Leader's voice calls out again.

'It is a new way. It is a better way.' His pressing nasal tone slices into the air, demanding our silence, making way for itself. I let the words fall on me, feel them stroke down along thirsty skin and tendons, settling around my throat. For this voice we left home and came to paradise. Now, only our bodies remain here, working, restlessly waiting for words to be turned into bread.

Someone claps their hands to signal a change to the line. We scramble into a new configuration and continue mindlessly passing from left to right. Take it and hand it along.

My former neighbour is now far away. I can see her whispering to a hollow-faced woman. Their shoulders touch, their heads tilt towards each other. My former neighbour's glazy eyes suddenly shoot up to the armed guard. She signals with a slight nod and the guard is upon the hollow-face, ripping her arms back so the bucket crashes and spills water on the thirsty earth. The woman's arms are limp under his tightening grip; her legs stumble and drag as she is escorted away for punishment. The hole she has left in the line closes seamlessly. The buckets continue. Take it and hand it along.

The first time I heard The Leader speak, I was thousands of miles from this place, in a white town hall that smelled like the harvest. Crickets buzzed on the other side of wooden walls as I sat in a crowd of people I had known since childhood. The Leader looked down at us from the stage and offered his words like a ladder.

'... and believe me when I say, I know the trials you have lived through. Day after day, existing to consume. A meaningless existence that ends up consuming you. I know the torture of your isolation. Individuality holds your spirit captive. You were not made for this life, you weary people. There is a new way. There is a better way. Reach out and experience the breadth. Plumb the depths and rise to new heights.'

As he spoke, his hair flopped from one side of his face to the other, pushed about by a solid hand. The other punctuated his words, his thumb and forefinger pinched together striking the air emphatically. His conviction gave him the haze of a man in the early stages of love. It appeared, in his eyes, we were not just a mottled, rural crowd perched warily on folding chairs, trying to understand long words in the dusk of a working day. He saw who we could become. As his words flowed on, it seemed as if there was no one else in the room. The sniffles and coughs, the sounds of shuffling seemed to disappear, consumed by his energy. It stretched out from the stage to coat my vision, smoothing the rough edges of walls and chairs, old clothes and grimy floorboards. It lent the dusty air an effervescence that filled me as I breathed in its glowing pieces.

The Leader approached me when the speech ended. He wore a simple collared shirt and large square glasses, the frames of which rested on fleshy cheeks. His eyes scanned from my sandals up and over my cotton dress, taking me in and locking onto my core.

'I can see you are a wise woman. So captivated by truth.' He took my hand in between his and tapped gently; the soft repetitive pressure of his fingers on the back of my hand spread peace. This was the miracle I needed, the one that anti-depressants hadn't been able to achieve. Nothing had been strong enough to plug the black hole, that vortex that sucked in all motivation and delight.

'How do I take hold of it?' I tightened my grip.

'You are a genuine soul. I can feel your dedication. Come and gather with us and I will teach you the way to freedom.'

'I've never heard…' I began, but The Leader had let my hand drop and moved on to speak with the young couple waiting behind him. I saw the Mackinlay's and their gaggle of children scamper to the door: Marg herding the kids, moving from shoulder to shoulder to shoulder as they tried to swerve and duck off; Bill shaking his head, striding away. I worried for him because I knew he was sad and he seemed such a reasonable person.

For a year I gathered with The Leader and his people before he revealed the plan. He described it to us on a Monday evening at the temple building on his property and by Friday we had left the country. Once I knew what he had waiting for us, the past faded like the outline of a stranger walking into the night.

When I told my husband, all those months ago, I had been singing and dancing around the kitchen bench:

And the truth will set you free from the pain of yourself. We are one. It is a new way. It is a better way.'

It was that time in the late afternoon when sparrows dominate the sky with their shifting formations.

'You seem happy?' he said as he walked through the front door.

'I've been happy for months.' I shimmied towards him with our younger daughter on my hip, bouncing her to the silent rhythm of the temple song. He put large, rough hands on my cheeks and pulled my face into a kiss.

'I know I don't get too involved in all that stuff but it's nice to see you like this.'

'*All that stuff* is the reason.' I tried to catch his eyes and show him the truth, but he looked at his dirty boots instead.

'How far off is dinner?' he asked, bending down over his shoelaces.

'Hey, we need to talk.'

'Darl, I'm really hungry. Can we –'

'This is important. The People are moving away.'

'Ah shit.' He looked up at me from the floor, propped on one knee like a man waiting for an answer. 'I'm sorry. That's gonna be tough on you.'

'What? No. It's the best thing that could happen for us.'

'Us? What are we talking about?'

'Moving.' I shifted my weight to the other hip, continued slowly, 'Us, moving to that compound in Geytan.' I brushed my daughter's soft fringe back from her face. My husband pinched the bridge of his nose.

'Fuck Jane.' He stood, reached over and took our daughter from my arms. 'That is not happening.' He ushered our children out of the room, closing their bedroom door. Through the narrowing doorway I could see them pottering around a faded Barbie dollhouse. 'I'd like you to consider starting treatment again Janey. I think it's –'

'That… that is not our way.' I breathed in and out deliberately, tapping my foot against the floor according to the sequence taught by The Leader. 'Darling, you've seen how different I am. You've got to know that it's real?'

'I know you're excited about all of it and I've been patient but –'

'Patient? A miracle happens and you need patience? You're a captive, you –'

'I won't let you take our girls.'

'I'm their mother.'

'Yeah, some of the time.'

We stood in silence.

'Look, Janey babe,' he said softly. 'I don't know a lot but...' He brought both hands up to rub his face. 'I see a guy with a lot of words.'

That was the moment I walked out of the room because it had begun: the blaspheming of The Leader, just like he said it would. Another sign that the move was needed. I walked into the bedroom to pack our bags.

'It's time to gather in the common place,' shouts a man and a gun. The heavy orange sun beats down on us. 'Time to gather.'

'It's a drill,' we murmur. 'It's another drill.' The words string along the line like fingers over prayer beads.

'I'm out,' I say to the gun. 'I stay on watch duty for –'

'To the common place, everybody!' It's long black nose presses into the soft place between my shoulder and breastbone. 'Everybody!'

'It's not a drill,' we say. 'This is not a drill,' we cry to one another, we cry to nobody.

My feet join the tangled movement of others. We trip over rocks and step on each other silently. I know this place. This trudging place, alone, next to all the bodies. I can feel the fury buried in shallow graves under their skin, ready to rise again if it wasn't for the machine guns. I remember the moments when we began to turn, moments nestled together under our ribs pushing up and up until we can't breathe.

We arrive in the open dirt space we call the common place. Old picnic tables circle the perimeter. This is where we sing and listen and obey.

'Do not tell the children.' The order comes through The Leader's teeth and spears the paralysed crowd. 'Do not upset them. They were not made for this world. We will pass over and meet in the other place and truly be united.' He chants this final sermon over the body of his dead wife. She lies next to the altar, an empty white cup by her hand. I see the Holloway's – mother, father, boy and baby. The mother is translucent and swaying gently, a jellyfish holding a screaming baby girl, eyes shut against the armed man with the white cups. The father has both arms spread around them in empty surrender. *This is not a drill.*

Reality winds back its brutal arm to punch me in the gut, forcing me to my knees. I see my children, their faces tucked safely into the last hidden space of my mind. I see the husband who took them and ran before I could bring them here. I pray that they find a new mother, a better mother. I look again at the cups and the crowd. I turn instead to face the waiting guns.

Habiba Cooper Diallo

Habiba Cooper Diallo was one of six finalists in the 2018 London Book Fair Pitch Competition. She self-published her first book, *Yeshialem Learns About Fistula*, and her work has been included in several anthologies. She is a women's health advocate and is passionate about bringing an end to a maternal health condition called obstetric fistula.

Desert Blues

She kept walking, tightening the indigo fabric around her body. There in the depths of the Sahara where sand blanketed the earth she noticed her dripping so much. So, she chose to walk at night when the blackness hid her shame. The moon was her compass. She thought of her life up until now. They had lost their baby. She, her fertility, her ability to walk properly, and her dignity too because the urine kept coming and she couldn't help that she was revolted by the smell of her own feces.

They met each other for the first time at their wedding. He promised he would love her. And he did. She wouldn't have chosen anyone else had she been able to choose. Sadio's soul was light and she knew that he really loved her. She could see it in the way his eyes softened whenever he looked at her. She had never known that anything could be more painful than her wedding night because a few years before, she was cut and then sewn so tightly that only a small space was left to allow urine and her monthly menses to flow. And then all at once her stitches opened and she had never felt so open before, but it was an uncomfortable kind of open. An open that made her remember the pain of losing her father. Of being told she could not go to school because she was a girl. Of having to queue for hours to receive millet flour and salt given to her family by the Americans. She remembered the way her uncles looted their house upon her father's death, taking everything except his prayer beads. Those beads, the only inheritance she had from him. She grasped them now, ran her fingers over them invoking the name of God – the merciful one. Rahman.

So when her belly started growing some weeks after their wedding, she promised that her baby girl would never be cut. That she would never know the pain of being closed, only to be opened again. Rugi had an unforgiving labour, a four-day labour. But on the fourth day, after forcing her way into the world, that sweet girl who had danced in her belly for nine months, was all at once still. Sadio said he was not sad at all, that it was the will of God. Though, Rugi could read the disappointment on his face. One morning, a couple of months after they had released their baby girl to the spirit world, Rugi woke up to a mattress that was wet. Soiled. Not just with urine but with feces too. Soon it was not only the constant dripping that tormented her, her right foot had become numb and she could barely walk. Sadio found a stick and gave it to her to use as a cane. He told her not to worry, that he would save enough money to take her to hospital where she would find help. She thought that things might just get better, until Sadio's parents told her she had to leave. They could not stand her smell and the fact that she had failed to give their son a child. They told Sadio that he must divorce her and find a new wife to have his children. But Sadio loved Rugi. They would go to the desert. First to Mali, then to Niger and onto Algeria from where they would be among thousands of migrants who would pay traffickers to get them into Europe. Lam-pe-dusa, he had told her. They would have a better life in Europe and she would find a doctor to make her dry again.

After crossing through Niger, they were handed over to a new group of traffickers, stern men in blue turbans. They refused to let Rugi onto the truck. Her smell revolted them and they would not travel the 2000 kilometres to Algeria with her in the back. "Take her or give us back our money!" Sadio had insisted. They refused. His pleas were lost to the abysses of the Sahara.

Sadio left Rugi in a small Tuareg village in Agadez. He would go to Algeria on his own and demand that those traffickers take them. They had to! They had taken their money! The chief had a tent pitched for Rugi at the edge of the village. The little ones would leave meals outside her tent and sneak coy glances her way, curious to know more about their visitor. Though, they dared not tarry, or else their mother Assalama would soon appear, warning that they would catch a disease from going too close to the sick woman. Eventually Assalama, who had scoffed at Rugi since her arrival, informed her that her condition could be treated in Nigeria. Weeks passed and then months. Sadio had not returned. He had promised he would come back for her, but it did not seem he was coming and she could not wait anymore. So, one day on the cusp of dusk, Rugi dressed in her indigo cloths, steadied herself on her cane and told Assalama that she would go to Nigeria. Assalama gave her an absent minded half nod and turned away as she hobbled into the night.

She did not know that even the wives of the pharaohs of old suffered what she was suffering. That a few hundred activists in Canada, Europe, and even in her own country were pressuring governments to act on her behalf. She did not know. How was a woman like her, gaunt, illiterate, disinherited to know? She was alone.

Obstetric fistula. That's what it was called. A hole in the birth canal caused by a complicated childbirth that left a woman without control of her urine or feces.

She arrived in the town of Maradi at the border between Niger and Nigeria. Two men sitting on a log observed her as she walked. It was not long before many people gathered to watch her, as a dotted trail of urine marked her path in the sand. A grey truck pulled up beside her. Nervous, she quickened her pace.

"Rugi!" A man jumped out of the truck and called out to her. She gasped and turned back to look at him. It was Sadio.

"What are you doing Rugi?"

"Sadio, I couldn't wait anymore. How did you find me?"

"When I went back for you, Assalama said you had left for Nigeria."

"What took you so long?"

"I'm sorry Rugi. When I went to Algeria, the traffickers still refused to take you. So, I had to work because I couldn't come back without enough money to get you to a doctor."

The driver told them to hurry up. He wanted to reach Katsina before nightfall. Sadio helped Rugi into the back of the truck and they crossed the border into Nigeria.

Aminu knew she was coming. As he fingered his prayer beads, he could see the loss of something. It was not a baby – that he could see was already gone – but the loss of something else. He continued stroking his beads. A desert flower blooming through parched earth suddenly withers. And then he saw her, limp and emaciated, draped in indigo fabric, the kind Aminu had seen his mother and grandmother wear, the fabric that had traversed the desert for hundreds of years on the bodies of his nomadic ancestors. Her husband stood anchored beside her, the fear in his eyes betraying his strength. It was the fear of not knowing, of wanting. A fear that Aminu had seen in so many of the families who came to the clinic to seek help.

"Honno inneteda?" he smiled and asked her name.

"Rugi," she met his eyes and steadied herself as much as her limp foot would allow.

He beckoned her and Sadio to follow him into the clinic.

Naja'atu, the nurse with the smiling eyes and bent nose spent the next two weeks feeding Rugi eggs, beans, and chicken to fortify her for surgery. She spoke to her in Fulani as Dr. Aminu had when she and Sadio arrived. Rugi was in awe. Her people where everywhere. In Fouta, where she came from, it was known that their people stretched as far as the famous Nile River. She had grown up hearing that from her grandmother and village elders. But, it was her first time to leave Fouta and discover the world that was beyond the rolling valleys and green mountains. They were a great tribe, a proud people who had conquered many and established empires. Yet, there she was, a Fulani woman who could not hold her bowels, poor, homeless, wretched. And she wondered if that's what it meant to be a great people.

On the day of the operation, Rugi was wheeled into a large room with whitewashed walls. There were screens and wires hooked up all around her. Everyone, including Sadio, wore light blue cotton shirts with matching trousers – the kind of clothing she had first seen health workers in her village wear when the Ebola disease devastated her country a few years earlier. Hours later, she awoke to a room ringing with excitement.

"Congratulations, you are dry Rugi!" Dr. Aminu cheered. Naja'atu clapped and Sadio's lips curved into a broad smile, his eyes glowing in jubilation.

"But Rugi," this time Dr. Aminu called her name so softly as if to not wake a sleeping child, "I have to tell you that you will not be able to have children anymore."

His words fell on her ears like sizzling balls of coal being dribbled through her flesh. The tears came like a quiet storm. Later that day, Sadio found her huddled in a corner of the courtyard, rocking back and forth, sobbing to herself in a hysterical murmur. He knelt down beside her and lay his head on her stomach. Indigo crept into the evening sky. "Rugiatu, the bearer of good things," Sadio whispered to her. "The bearer of joy. Rugi, Sadio's girl, Sadio's love, the one who makes Sadio smile. Rugi, the bearer of life."

Fiona Ennis

Fiona Ennis holds a BA in English and Philosophy and an MA in English Literature and Publishing from National University of Ireland, Galway. She has a PhD in Philosophy from University College Cork. She lectures in Literature and Philosophy in Waterford Institute of Technology. She won the Molly Keane Creative Writing Award 2019. Her fiction has been published in *Sonder* and will be included in the forthcoming *Leicester Writes Anthology*, published by Dahlia Books. Her poetry has been published in *The Honest Ulsterman*. She has read her short fiction at literary festivals including the *Immrama Festival* and *Waterford Writers' Weekend*.

Host

Elodie walked along the canal path, her feet squelching in her trainers. It was early evening, too early to go back to the tent, but her hoodie was soaked from the rain, and she was looking forward to wrapping herself in her Mum's camel wool coat. When it got wet, it became musty, but once it was dry, it kept out the worst of the biting November cold. At least the tent was rain-proof, for now. She tried not to hang out in it during the day; Conor had been good enough to take her in and share it at night with her, and it's not as if he'd known her that well. It was getting pretty cluttered in there with all their stuff, and the last time she'd gone back, she'd found all her things piled on her sleeping bag, including her black sack of washing.

Shivering, she took a foil bag from her pocket and lifted out a sausage. Even in the driving rain, the queue at St. Paul's soup kitchen had gone around the block. Just as well she'd had enough for the marked down stuff from the hot food counter in Costway. The wedges had been spicy and soggy, but the sausage was dark brown and shrivelled, and when she bit it, the skin cracked. Back when she was growing up in Ranelagh, her mum used to laugh at the small Irish sausages, and on the rare sunny days, would place a large ring of Toulouse sausage on the barbeque, which made the fire spit.

Then she'd say, 'Elodie, now that is a sausage, non? Not like the things we get here.' It was always the same words.

The rain pattered on the canal and, off the path, near the wall, were the tents. Most of them were those piss-poor ones, sold for festivals, wouldn't keep anything out, a bit like the one her mum had set up for the two of them to play 'camping,' in their garden, back when Elodie was a child and hadn't been invited to another sleepover. The ones by the canal had been donated. The lads living in them were always giving out about having to sleep in puddles when the rain came, and a woman who'd slept in one had died of pneumonia. She'd collapsed while begging outside of the GPO, and nobody had helped her for a while as they'd thought it was some kind of stunt, so she could rob them or something. Not long after, she'd died in hospital; well, that's what was said anyway. Someone else had her tent now, some guy with two dogs.

At least Conor's tent was sturdy. She coughed outside it, waited a moment before unzipping the outer door, the 'porch door' as he called it, took off her trainers and lined them up near his boots. Then she took off her socks. Her toes felt numb, and she tried to curl them on the base-sheet of the tent to get some warmth back in. When she opened the zip into the main section, the battery-operated light was on, and Conor nodded. She opened her belt and slipped it out of the loops, then peeled off the jeans and wet hoodie and put them in her black bag of washing. Conor didn't like damp things being left around the tent.

She could feel his eyes on her as she dried herself with her old towel, but things had cooled down a lot on that front, just the odd blow job here or there, nothing like the awful intensity of when she'd first stayed in the tent. He wasn't her type, not at all, but with him, she felt a bit safer. Staying by herself, under a flimsy piece of canvas, with only a zip or two between her and whoever'd get in, wasn't something she could do. On the few times Conor had left the tent at night, only for a little while, she'd lain there, eyes open, her arms outside the sleeping bag in case she needed to use them, her fingers digging into her palms. So, it was either close her eyes and get on with it or go back to the hostel. The last time she'd had a shower was there, and she hadn't wanted to get out of the hot water. Since then, whenever she wanted to wash herself, she sneaked into the disabled toilet in the Travelodge. The last time, when she'd stripped down and was washing herself at the sink with the citrus handwash, even that had been cut short by a rapping at the door. After drying herself and dressing, she'd opened the door to a lady with a walking frame being helped in by a young woman, and as the door closed, Elodie hoped she hadn't splashed the floor. Growing up, her mum used to always give out to her for splashing water onto the ceramic tiles outside the bath.

Back in the hostel, there'd been no shampoo or conditioner, just Aldi shower gel, and it had taken her ages afterwards to get the knots out of her hair. When she'd gone back to the dorm, the girl on the bunk opposite was sitting on blood-speckled sheets, with her trousers pulled down, tapping her thigh, about to shoot up. The blanket and sheet on Elodie's bunk had been pulled back; the synthetic pillow had been moved, and another woman sat on the mattress. She'd looked at the rucksack on Elodie's shoulder and got up. Elodie had run out of the dorm, down the stairs onto the street.

There was none of that trouble with Conor. She put on a jumper, then gave her feet a good rub with the towel and pulled on some leggings and her last pair of dry socks. The towel smelled musty, and she put it in the black sack. The next day, or maybe the day after, she'd have to go to the petrol station and put on a wash in a machine there. It was a good bit cheaper than the launderette, and hopefully she'd make enough from begging to put on a load. She'd better check the drum in the machine this time though. The last time she'd used one, her clothes had come out covered in dog hair. Conor said some people used them to wash pet bedding. She wrapped herself in her mum's coat, then climbed into her sleeping bag. Wriggling to warm herself, she was careful not to touch the inner layer of the tent off the flysheet or turn her face towards Conor. Then she closed her eyes and pretended to sleep.

She woke up. It was dark outside the tent, and the battery light remained on. Someone rustled at the entrance, and the zip to the porch came down.

A girl's voice said, 'Conor?'

He said, 'Tina?'

The zip to the main part of the tent opened, and a young woman clambered in, dripping. Mascara dribbled down her cheek from a bloodshot eye that kept blinking. Her lip was crusted with blood.

Conor said, 'He do that to you?'

Elodie had never heard him use that tone.

Tina nodded.

'You made some choice.'

Tina was staring at Elodie, and when Elodie pushed her hair back from her face, grease transferred to her fingers.

Conor said, 'Tina and I go way back,' and patted the sleeping bag. Tina sat beside him, and her wet skinny jeans must have soaked it, but he didn't seem to mind.

Tina's eyes moved around the tent. 'Any chance I could lie low for a bit, just 'til I get sorted?'

There was barely any space between the sleeping bags as it was.

Tina said, 'Look, he knows where me mates live.'

Conor said, 'You can stay. I've a dry jumper and tracksuit pants if you want to throw them on. They'll be massive on you, but you can't wear anything wet in the tent.'

'Thanks.'

Elodie kept her eyes on Conor, and he pretended not to watch as Tina took off her sweatshirt. When she tried to yank down her skinny jeans, they were wet and clung to her, and as she sat there in her orange panties trying to pull them over her thighs, she laughed.

'Ah, Conor. Give us a hand, will ya?'

Conor nodded at Elodie. 'Can you scoot for a while?'

Elodie climbed out of the entrance. The rain had stopped.

She walked back along the canal path to the tent. The lapels of her mum's coat kept her neck and part of her cheeks warm, but her nose was frozen. Above the wall, the streetlights from the nearby estate sent out enough light for her to make her way. Some of the people who lived in the estate were sound; a few of them would drop down food that was on the turn, that kind of thing, but most of them just avoided the area, not that it was dodgy or anything, but they didn't know that, and it could get noisy. Most of them staying in the tents tried to keep the place someway straight, didn't draw attention to themselves, and the red-haired garda and the little blonde one usually left them alone.

When she reached the tent, she pretended to have a fit of coughing, then opened the porch door zip and took off her trainers. Conor's boots and Tina's trainers sat alongside each other, and Tina's white socks lay beside her runners, stretched out. They were those little ones that couldn't be seen when you had trainers on, no ankles on them at all. When Elodie got into the main part of the tent, Conor's sleeping bag was unzipped and partly covered him and Tina. They were fully clothed, and Conor spooned Tina, his arm across her, his face snuggled into her hair. Tina looked up when Elodie came in and stroked Conor's arm. Elodie drank some water, turned off the battery light, clambered across to her sleeping bag and felt her way into it. Tina pushed back against her as she zipped it up; there was only enough room for Elodie to sleep on her side.

The next morning, rain pattered on the side of the tent, and Elodie needed to pee. She unzipped her sleeping bag and crawled along the tent trying not to climb over Tina or Conor's legs. They were still clothed, Conor wrapped around Tina, who was in foetal position. Elodie stared at them for a moment, took off her mum's coat and pulled on a hoodie.

The nearest thick bushes were a good few minutes away, and the grass squelched underfoot as she walked to the path, trying not to slip. No one was outside the tents, but as she passed one of them, a dog barked, and someone roared at it to keep quiet. Above the wall, lights were on in some of the houses. She was glad she couldn't smell freshly brewed coffee. At the weekends, when she was a child, she and her mum would have pain au chocolat at weekends. Back when Elodie was ten, and her mum had felt low and was stretched out on the couch in her dirty dressing gown, Elodie had sat at the table in her school uniform and eaten pain au chocolat for dinner three days in a row.

When she got back to the tent, Elodie opened the porch zip. The zip to the main part of the tent was closed. Lined up in the porch was her black sack of washing and her big rucksack. Her sleeping-bag was rolled up and held together with her belt. She looked at her stuff, all her stuff, for a full minute. There was no sound of anything moving inside the main part of the tent, but when she stuffed her black sack into her rucksack, she heard someone shift inside the tent, and she paused. It went quiet again, and she fitted the sleeping bag under the rucksack's flap, and pulled the straps tight, the ends of the sleeping bag flopping over the sides. Her hand pushed the zip to the main part of the tent slightly forward, then nudged it back. She gathered up her stuff and trudged back along the canal path.

The last time she'd been thrown out, from the house she'd lived in with her mum, the clothes she'd packed hadn't been too clean either, not that she'd cared. It was just one more thing she'd let slip, along with the rent and everything else. Standing on the pavement outside their home, everything she owned in her large rucksack, she'd looked at the landlord who'd stood inside their living room window. Well, it had never really been their home; her mum had found Irish people's obsession with owning their own home strange and had always rented. Their landlord hadn't even hidden behind the curtain but had stayed at the window watching her. Elodie was sorry she'd ever tried to clean up that grout between his tiles, even though the stain still sat in the grooves. She'd really tried to get rid of the blood stain, but it just wouldn't budge, not even when she'd scrubbed it with a nail-brush until her nails were broken.

Months before that, on the day she'd found her mum in the bath, she hadn't paid much attention to the grout, but the blood on the ceramic tiles had wiped away easily with a fluffy bath-towel, and when she'd dumped it, she'd felt bad she hadn't used newspaper. A police-woman had told her she shouldn't have cleaned up the mess.

Earlier that afternoon, her mum had rung her twice at work, but Elodie had taken whingey calls all day long at the call centre, so when she'd had a few precious minutes of a toilet break, she hadn't returned the call. Her mum spent every day on the couch, staring at the wall, the telly blaring, and whenever she did speak, she was so low, Elodie hadn't the energy anymore to rally her. After work that evening, when Elodie had let herself into the house, and saw the couch was empty and the telly was off, she'd paused before going up the stairs.

'Mum?'

There was no answer. She could hear the drone of the bathroom fan; the light was on and the door was open, which wasn't like her mum, even when she was unwell. They weren't the kind of people not to close the bathroom door. Her mum was draped in the bath, her left arm dangling over the side, blood dribbling down her wrist and along the curve of her hand. Her hair was wet and tied up in a butterfly clip. She'd gone to the trouble of washing her hair. Before that, she hadn't washed her hair all week.

But she hadn't taken the trouble to write a note, even though for months afterwards Elodie had checked in drawers and handbags in case she'd missed it. Elodie didn't use her phone much afterwards, just kept staring at the two missed calls and reading texts from when her mum was well. Her boss at the call centre must have tired of her not even bothering to ring in, and soon her mum's family in Toulouse stopped ringing and ringing and ringing. When she absolutely had to go to the shop, she'd go when it was dark. She couldn't bear bumping into anyone that knew her or her mother.

When she did, some woman would always cock her head to one side and say, 'How aaaarrre you?'

After some months, the ESB had been cut off. Elodie couldn't even boil the kettle or store milk in the fridge, so she just drank water, and rinsed the same mug every day. She couldn't face washing the pile of dirty plates and cups that sat in the sink and were heaped all over the draining board. One day she began to, but the water was freezing, and she gave up after she'd washed the orange sauce from a plate that had held spaghetti hoops.

The landlord sometimes came by at night, banging on the door, and when he finally managed to kick her out, one of her neighbours had seen her on the footpath with her rucksack and brought her to the Social Welfare Office. Then she'd let her sleep on her couch for a night, even though Elodie heard her row with her husband about it. Their living room was just under their bedroom. The next day, her neighbour drove her to houses with vacant rooms, but when the fifth landlord refused to take her and, like the others, said he preferred cash to getting paid by Social Welfare, her neighbour had dropped her to the homeless hostel and pressed forty euros into her hand.

The evening after she was kicked out of the tent, the sky was dishwater grey, and Elodie trudged past Supermac's. She'd had tomato soup at St. Paul's, but they'd run out of bread, and the smell of chips and burgers made her stomach gurgle. All she'd made begging was eighty cents. In the window was a birthday party, and the little girls had their faces painted as tigers. When one of them saw Elodie look in the window, she pawed at the glass and made faces. A woman made her turn around, licked her napkin and cleaned some ketchup off the little girl's cheek.

Elodie waited outside the back of the shopping centre for the last clink of the metal shutter to come down and then undid the straps of her rucksack. The awning had gaps which let some rain through;

Fiona Ennis

Conor had said it was designed like that to prevent people like them
sleeping there. There was a security camera though, tilted towards
the door, so it felt a bit safer than other spots. She looked down the
street, then took out her sleeping bag, still held together by the belt,
and leaned it against a dry spot in the corner. The ground was damp
under the awning, and she tipped all the dirty clothes from her black
sack into her rucksack. She needed to put the black sack under her
sleeping bag to protect it from damp, and there was no point in using
the sack to separate clothes anymore; nothing she had was clean. It
wasn't long enough, so she stretched a dirty hoodie under the sleeping
bag, climbed in and zipped it up. In the next street, there was a thud,
followed by a bang, and she lay still until all went quiet again. She
wriggled around to get warm, but then sat upright and rummaged
through her rucksack, before emptying everything onto the ground.
Even though she knew her mum's camel coat wasn't there, she kept
sifting through the damp clothes.

Carol Farrelly

Carol Farrelly is currently working on a short story collection and a novel. Her stories have been widely published in journals, and broadcast on BBC Radio 4. She has been shortlisted for the Society of Authors' ALCS Tom-Gallon Trust Award, the Bridport Prize, Fish Prize and RA & Pin Drop Short Story Award. Creative Scotland awarded her a Robert Louis Stevenson Fellowship. She is also a previous Jerwood/Arvon mentee. She has a DPhil on Thomas Hardy's fiction. She spent one dreamy year in Italy and is in love with all things Venetian.

Clipped

The cows had the man and his dog cornered against the far drystone wall. Fran unzipped her hoodie and leant upon the gate, in the shade of the old pear tree. Here was something rich to watch.

Usually, come mid-autumn – the calves' sturdy season – the mothers didn't bat an eyelid at any walkers. The endless parade of fluorescent jackets didn't seem to mither them, nor the stopping and squinting and yelping at Google maps, which turned every dale and pasture and footpath into blank white space. This man, however, had lumbered rather than filed across the field, and the retriever had strained at her leash and barked at the young ones – and so the mothers' nerves jangled.

A wall of brown muscle, the cows shifted another inch closer to the man and dog. The gate rattled as Fran leant down harder. She should shout the man instructions. *Let the bleeding dog go. Don't harbour the threat.* But she didn't have the will – or the forgiveness – in her yet.

He shouldn't need telling, in any case. He might not be a farming man, but he was no blow-in. He'd lived hereabouts all his life; and he was old enough to be her father. You don't take a dog near calves. Everyone learned that knee-high around here. You don't stir the mother's blood. But if, somehow, you sleepwalked yourself into a mob of cows, then you knew to ignore the townie instructions nailed to every gate. You let your dog off the leash.

'Raven,' he said to the dog. 'Good girl. Stay.'

Fran winced. She'd never thought that name right. The first time she'd heard it, ten or more years ago, she'd winced too. The man had been nattering to the lollipop woman outside the high school gates. Raven, he kept saying. Raven, he crooned. Fran had looked up to the blossomy hawthorn tree and then the church roof opposite and then the sky. She saw a sparrow on a branch and three magpies skittering on tiles but no raven. Only when she stood beside them, to nudge the lollipop woman into action, did she see the black pup cradled in his arms. And she was the size of a chuffing raven, right enough. And Fran had understood the likeness: the feathery darkness, the corvid intelligence in the eye. The name, though, was wrong. Raven. As if the man intended to tame flight.

'Shoo.' The man flapped his anoraked arms.

Fran stepped back and looked up to the pear tree. One thin green fruit hung above her, still tight against the branch. If she twisted the stalk, it would resist, like sinew. Not ready yet, it would say. No sugary juices inside. No rich, white, slopping flesh.

'Away you go,' the man muttered.

The cows didn't budge. He pressed his shoulders against the wall and stretched his arms across the coping stones. He meant to signal surrender, perhaps, but it looked more like nonchalance to her – a drowsy rambler on a hot day who hoped this resilience of stones might soften into an armchair. From what she knew of him, that would fit. Listen here, lasses, he might be saying to the worried animals. You've got this all wrong. I meant no harm.

'Bugger off.' The man flapped again.

The cows huddled closer. Their hooves made a sound like molars grinding. The dog hunkered down and bared her teeth. Fran rubbed her thumb against a splinter on the gatepost. *Let the dog go*, she should shout. *Edge towards the gap stile. And whatever you do, don't turn your back on them.*

'Christ,' the man muttered.

Fran stayed in the tree's shadow and kept silent. She'd never liked the man, even before she'd landed on a good reason. The dislike had started with her mother, who would always fall quiet when he passed them in the village. If he happened to be with his pretty but po-faced wife, the three adults would nod at each other. If he was alone, he'd venture a quiet 'hello' and her mother would nod while squeezing Fran's hand tighter or, as she grew older, linking her arm. Stay, her touch said.

The day Mum first saw him with the dog, a squiggle of fur, she actually gasped. 'So he can look after a pup,' she'd muttered, once they were around the corner. 'He can own a pup, at least.' That was when the thought first came to Fran: the good reason to dislike the man.

He was rummaging in his jacket pocket now. He pulled out a phone and jabbed at the screen, as though there might be a rescue button. Swipe up to go home.

Raven looked up at her master and whined. She wanted his instruction to fly. If only he'd unloose her, she'd throw herself against these soft-eyed assailants and their tumult of jaws and hooves.

The phone fell from his hand and slapped onto the muck beneath the cows' legs. 'Shit,' he muttered

The bulkiest cow lowered her head and tested one hoof against the phone's flashing screen. Crack. Her tail whipped side to side.

The man finally showed some sense and wheeled windmill arms at the cows, which did make them pause. Make yourself big, her mother had always told her. Don't show fear.

Fran wondered what had brought the man out this far, five miles from the village. She'd only ever seen him on pavements before and some of the gentler, signposted bridleways. He'd never once come near their house, as far as she knew – although she had pictured it occasionally. He would have been younger then, when he visited. Dark-haired. Handsome, probably. Mum would have been living alone, a young woman managing a small farmhouse more or less by herself. People back then, Mum said, had called her all sorts. Plucky. Crazy. Sad. Only child of a divorced, failing farmer who hanged himself. A little decent plot of milk and honey for a willing young man, some said.

Perhaps, all these years later, the man had finally made his return. The news had rustled around the village that her mother was ill. Locals called her plucky and sad again. And still crazy. Refusing hospital treatment. The apple doesn't fall far, Fran had heard Mrs Clough whisper in the Co-op the other day. A few of the kinder folk had dropped by with casseroles and pies and loaves of dough to rise in the oven whenever they had need. The man must have heard the news too. Perhaps he'd also come bearing gifts – or a long overdue apology.

The cows snorted. Steam rose from their flanks. Midges and pollen swirled.

Fran reached up into the tree and squeezed the dangling pear. It was firm to the fingertips, even around the stem. She'd been right. Not quite ready yet. Perhaps, in a few weeks, she could pluck and pulp them and brew them into perry. They could both do with some cheap booze.

Fran looked over her shoulder and saw the blue wire of smoke from her and her mother's farmhouse, faint in the distance. Even though this autumn was proving mild, they built a fire every day now. The cancer had made Mum too weak for the outdoors, but she craved normality inside. The casseroles and dough lay untouched in the freezer. Every afternoon, Mum made a crumble or pie or stew. Every morning, she sent Fran out for more flour or sugar or fruit – especially lemons. A trickle of lemon juice always made a difference. Fran wondered if these pears would turn sweet enough in time for Mum.

'Hello!' the man cried. 'Is that you?'

Fran turned back. The cows' arched haunches hid him from view. It must be her he was calling, though.

'Sarah Harker's daughter?' he asked.

She stood on tiptoe, grabbed the pear and twisted the stalk ninety degrees. It didn't loosen. She still said nothing.

'Hello!' he shouted. 'Please. Hello?'

The dog whined.

Fran climbed onto the first rung of the gate.

'Thank god,' the man groaned. His face was pale as her mother's. 'Can you help us?'

Raven pulled against the leash and stared her bright black eyes at Fran. She wondered if the dog remembered her. Once, Fran had taken her for a walk, without permission. It was years ago now. She'd seen Raven roaming the village several days in a row, looping the green, wandering after strangers. The man, Fran thought, must have put her out on the streets to turn feral or become roadkill. He's grown tired of the responsibility, her mother said when she went home and told her. Thoughtless bugger. Even a dog's too much for his feeble sort. A few days later, they found out his wife had upped and left him. Gone to London to live with her single sister. Her mother went quiet at that news.

It was Raven, though, who had come to Fran. She had bounded towards her, wet-nosed and shiny-eyed – and so they'd gone on her favourite walk towards the old viaduct. Fran's stride gave the dog a compass and a companion; and the reverse had also been true. A good stretch of the haunches and the eyes. A soft paw and soft hand. For good parts of the walk, they'd stepped in rhythm. Sleepers in the same bed, she'd heard, breathed to the same beat. Women in the same house bled on the same days of the month: lovers, friends, and even mothers and daughters – if they were close.

When they'd reached the viaduct, they ignored the danger signs and walked along the bridge. People had abseiled down the columns only the week before. Raven and she leaned over the parapet and looked down to the road climbing away from the river, and for a moment she imagined the bridge giving way beneath them. A cyclist would find them lying on the road, two piles of shattered bones. 'The dog must have gone after her,' the cyclist would say down the pub, afterwards. 'That's real devotion for you.' The landlady would tilt a glass of ale against the tap and say, 'or maybe it was the other way round.'

When Fran and Raven had returned to the village, the man was looking out from his window. He nodded as she approached the gate. Perhaps he thought she'd found the dog wandering and brought her home. Or perhaps he thought it fitting that Sarah Harker's daughter should walk the pent-up neglect out of his dog. An exorcism of sorts; and an admission. She'd always imagined him slinking away when her mother told him the news beneath the farmhouse eaves. Perhaps they'd just shagged against the lukewarm, white walls before she told him. 'But I'm married,' he would have said. 'I can't have another woman's child.' Maybe he'd even used the word 'own'. I can't own your child. Then he'd sent a craven text or two that night, from a darkened bathroom.

'If you insist on having it, I'll send money. Nothing more.' He'd used the word 'it', which was surely another reason her mother had refused his help. Now, no children to own from his failed marriage, a pang of regret bothered him.

The day after she'd borrowed his dog, the man reappeared in the village with Raven at his heels, collared in a tight leash. That was how it had been ever since. The dog was always four bound feet from his ankles, feathers clipped. 'That's what he wishes he'd done to his poor wife,' Mum said at the dinner table that night. 'Clipped her. That's what marriage makes of most folk. Owners and pets. Plucks out generosity in one and wildness in the other. We're better off out of it – aren't we, my love?'

Fran had flinched. She'd wondered if she'd got everything back-to-front. Her mother had been the one to refuse his pleas to become a family. She'd decided from the start to keep Fran fatherless. Not once had she ever asked if she missed having another parent. It's common enough, she always said. Plenty of animals raise their young ones alone. It had been such a solitary raising, though. Like polar bears cooped up for one never-ending winter in their snow cave. And most animals, she'd wanted to reply, let their young spring the gate quick. Sometimes, she feared Mum had never even told the man she was his. He'd only wondered that afternoon when she returned his dog and her dark hair and green eyes flashed.

'Help!' His voice was hoarse now. 'Please get us help.'

Fran climbed another rung of the gate. The hinges creaked. The sturdiest cow turned her head and batted blonde eyelashes at her. Raven yapped.

'Let the dog go,' she said. 'It's her that worries them.'

The man gave her a blank look. 'They'll trample her.'

The cows shuffled closer together, their tails flicking faster. One hooved kick and they might break the man's shin or puncture his liver.

'And they'll trample you,' she said, 'if you don't.'

The man pulled at the leash. Raven rubbed her head against his leg, while swiping a paw at the cows. Her instincts were crossed, like tangled puppet wires.

'Let her run away,' Fran explained. 'That'll calm them – or distract them. Then edge your way to the stile.'

He shook his head. 'She won't leave my side. She's loyal.'

Fran heard her mother's words again. An infantilised pet, in need of rewilding.

She climbed the third rung and cleared her throat. 'How do you know my name?'

He looked puzzled.

'How do you know my mother?' she repeated.

The pear tree creaked.

'Were you together once?'

'What?'

'A couple?'

'Me with your mother? Jesus. No.' It sounded almost drunken, his laugh. 'Are you crazy? Like her and – ' He stopped and tugged at his collar. 'Look, please, can you just help? My legs can't bear this much longer.'

'You didn't know her?' Fran asked.

'Barely.' He paused. 'I knew of her.'

Of her. Fran's foot slipped against the gate's rung. *Of her.* Like a rumour. Or a book you'd never want to read. Or a place that showed only arctic-white on your map. She fell backwards and hit the tree's arm-thick roots. She looked up into the arching branches and saw that lowest hanging pear. She wished she'd tugged at the stalk until she'd freed the fruit. It would be good to taste such sourness now.

The cows bayed.

'Let the dog go,' she said.

Hooves stamped against the earth. Stones thudded onto the mud. Chocks and hearting scattered like rubble. She imagined a cairn of coping stones rising in the field. The dog leapt over the rattling gate and bounded past her. A moment later, the man followed, no leash in his hand. She tilted her head and saw the blue smoke coiling into the upside-down sky.

Fran shut her eyes.

'Let her go,' she said.

Steven Fromm

Steven Fromm was born and raised in Detroit, Mich. He is a journalist, currently residing in New Jersey. His work has appeared in Salamander, Juxtaprose, The Ocotillo Review, The Columbia Journal and The Midwest Review. He is the 2020 winner of the Midwest Review's Greater Midwest Fiction Contest.

Six Carp

Claire sat quietly at the kitchen table with her laptop, methodically attempting to break into her husband's life.

She had a system. After writing down five possible passwords, she'd enter them into his email portal. She had to keep it to five tries at a time to avoid a lockout, wait an hour, then move on to the next five.

She scribbled on a yellow legal pad as she rummaged through the names of long-dead pets, vacation spots, sports teams, parents' middle names, favorite movies, actors, singers, songs, book titles and, yes, the first names of his old girlfriends.

She tried affixing some of them with numbers: birth dates, old street addresses, anniversaries, favorite ball players' batting averages (obtained via Google), death dates (their parents'), even the flight numbers from their recent trip to Vegas (from a remnant ticket in her scrapbook).

Nothing worked.

Her phone pinged. It was a text from Trent.

how are u?

She texted back a thumbs-up emoji. She preferred answering him in emojis when she was angry. It relayed a sense of curtness.

she come yet?

no. she said about 10. where are u?

layover. hit connect in 30

She shot him another thumbs-up emoji. He answered with a kissy face. Jesus.

Claire put down her phone and picked up her coffee mug. She looked out the kitchen window, across the road to their neighbor. Mr. Baughman was on his riding mower, pipe clenched in teeth, orbiting his front lawn in steadily diminishing oblong circles. He did it every Saturday morning. Trent would have been doing the same on their lawn, but he'd taken a flight out of town earlier that morning. It was an unexpected business trip to his company's L.A. division. He'd had three sudden L.A. trips in the last six weeks.

A beige Toyota passed on the road, slowing in front of the house. For a moment Claire thought the visitor had arrived early, but the car moved on.

Claire took another sip of coffee and looked down at the burgeoning scrawl of names and numbers on the legal pad, each triggering a grainy image from their shared history. Three more tries in this round. She put down her coffee mug and typed in Doris0426 (her mother's middle name, plus the numbers for April 26, the date Claire and Trent met). Nothing. Next came Hitchcock1846 (the name of their first dog, plus the address of their first apartment). Nothing. The last was DallasWhitford34 (the city of Trent's birth, the name of his childhood street, plus the Jersey number of David Ortiz, Trent's favorite ballplayer). Again, nothing.

She picked up her coffee. It felt cold. She went to the sink, tipped the mug, then refilled it from the pot. She didn't want more, but it was something to do. She looked at her watch. Fifty-seven minutes until the next round. She tried to remember how many rounds she'd burned through since Trent left that morning. Maybe three.

Claire knew the chances of hitting an alphanumeric password of up to 8 characters was right up there with lottery wins and lightning strikes. But she had an abiding faith in numbers and probability, a certainty that they'd yield their secrets if coaxed with the right combination of evaluation and insight. She'd made a good living from them for years as a statistician. Binomial coefficients. Nonlinear association. Random variables. And now passwords.

Breaking passwords.

She glanced at her watch again. Forty-six minutes until the next round. She started writing down the next five possibilities. Marlow611 (the name of a parrot Trent owned before they met, plus the street number of his office); Barnes1899 (the name of his favorite literary character, plus Hemingway's year of birth); Havens1969 (for one of his favorite performers, Richie Havens, opening act for Woodstock, plus the year).

Her phone pinged. She expected it to be another text from Trent, but it was from the visitor. Trent had given her Claire's number before he left.

be there in a bit. Anna.

Claire thought of replying with another thumbs-up, but stopped herself. She fired off a quick *Ok.*

Anna had lived in their home about eight years ago, two owners back, before relocating to the southern part of the state. She'd initially contacted Trent the week before last, saying she'd be in town for a conference, and wanted to drop by to see her old home.

"How'd she find our name?" Claire had asked.

"She said she was a realtor," Trent said. "They've got all those apps."

"Apps?"

"You know. They can tap into public records. Press a few buttons and our lives spill out." He waited a few moments and then intoned: "Privacy is dead."

Trent was fond of intoning. In the early years of their marriage, she interpreted it as some kind of wisdom. Now it sounded stagy, like he was quoting from a *New Yorker* article he didn't quite finish.

"So this woman contacts you out of the blue two weeks ago, asks if she can drop by, you say yes, then manage to bolt out of town the day before she comes?"

"I'm not *bolting* anywhere," Trent said. "Something came up in L.A. They asked me to troubleshoot."

"And you said yes. Again."

"Yes. I said Yes. Again. That's what employees do when their bosses get in a bind."

"Since when is a regional manager an employee?"

"Since the regional manager has a boss. And his boss has a boss. We've *all* got bosses."

"Ok. We've all got bosses. And while you're troubleshooting out in L.A. for your boss, some stranger is coming to our house."

"She's not a stranger."

"*Excuse* me?"

"She's not *exactly* a stranger. She lived in the house. We know who she is."

"Easy for you to say. You won't be here."

"C'mon. It's not like some *guy* is coming over."

She looked at him, trying to decide how to react. He was off to L.A. Again. But it was no problem, because it wasn't a *guy*. She felt something then. For the first time. Dislike. Fundamental dislike.

"Look," he said, his tone softer, "I'll be in touch with you the whole time."

"How reassuring. Our house will be on fire, and you'll be 10,000 feet over Cleveland."

He laughed at that. She didn't.

Thirty-five minutes to go until the next round. She wrote down Arturo0505. It was for Arturo's, the restaurant where they went for their first date, on a May 5. It was a longshot. His old password, before he changed it about two weeks ago, had been arturo@us. She'd tried to log on with it when he was off on his second troubleshooting trip. It didn't work. Up until then they'd known each other's email, Amazon and AmEx passwords, along with the PIN numbers of their bank accounts. She was on the verge of asking him about it when the latest trip to L.A. came out of nowhere. She'd decided to keep silent, and attempt to guess his new one. Lottery wins and lightning strikes aside, it was something to grasp onto at that moment as she sat in her kitchen waiting for a stranger to arrive while her husband hurtled toward the West Coast.

Twenty-nine minutes. Claire jotted down another one: BlackBolt03, after the Black Bolt, his favorite comic book character, plus 03 for the number of the issue he owned. Bowl213 came next. It was for bowling, one of Trent's many fleeting interests. The 213 was for this lifetime high score. He'd mentioned it more than once.

Another car passed. A black Subaru. Mr. Baughman was done mowing his lawn, and had moved on to cutting the hedges in front of his bay window. Claire glanced at the upper-right-hand corner of her screen. Twenty minutes. There was a chance she could get in one more set of tries before the woman arrived.

Claire thought of what would happen if she actually beat the math and hit on his password. He may have set up a two-step verification, which would require yet another password. But she dismissed her concern. It was the type of precaution she'd take, not him. He also might get an email notifying him that his account was being viewed from a different browser. It wouldn't matter. If she found what she suspected, the apologies and alibis wouldn't be coming from her. She thought of what he'd said: *privacy is dead*. She smiled for the first time in days.

Another car passed, this time a light blue Prius. It slowed, then moved on. Sixteen minutes. Claire wrote down glencoe621, after the name of their street and the date they'd moved in, June 21, three years ago. Three years. She looked around her at all the things they'd changed since then: kitchen counters, cabinets, appliances. And then beyond the kitchen: wall paper, paint, carpeting, windows, interior doors, even the landscaping for the front and back yards. The execution of each renovation had given them a certain energy and purpose. And then they'd stopped.

Claire remembered when it ended, after they finished upgrading the master bathroom about one year ago. Trent came home from work the day the contractor laid the last tile, surveyed the job, then turned to Claire with a grin.

"Now what?" he said.

She smiled, but had no answer. The house had been subdued.

Now what?

The light blue Prius passed again, slowed, then moved on. Claire got up, went to the kitchen window and watched the car go down the street. Mr. Baughman had finished his hedges and was walking toward the mailbox, pipe still in his mouth. Claire sat back down. Eleven minutes. She'd start with the Arturo's password, then go with Glencoe.

The Prius appeared again, slowed, passed and then went into reverse. It stopped in front of Claire's house. Eight minutes to go. The fourth round would have to wait.

Claire watched as Anna emerged from the car and closed the door. Mr. Baughman was at his mailbox, clutching some magazines. Anna turned and nodded at Mr. Baughman. He nodded back, but said nothing. She started walking toward the front door of Claire's house, but Claire wasn't watching her. She was looking at Mr. Baughman. He stood perfectly still, staring at Anna, the only movement a wisp of smoke rising from his pipe.

Claire shifted her look from Baughman to Anna. She was trim with short, dark hair highlighted by streaks of grey that stood out in the afternoon light. She wore an olive top and black, Athleta-style tights. Claire quickly logged off, closed the laptop, went to the front door and opened it. Anna was waiting. She hadn't bothered with the doorbell. She'd seen Claire in the window. They smiled at each other through the outer screen door.

"Anna?"

"Yes. Claire?"

Claire opened the screen door and Anna stepped in.

"I'd ask you if you had any problem finding us, but - "

They both laughed. It was the best ice-breaker Claire could think of.

"I hope this isn't too much of an intrusion, your husband said - "

" – not at all. Sorry he couldn't be here."

"Would love to have met him. He was called out of town?"

"*Suddenly*," Claire said.

Her tone came out sharper than she'd intended. Anna didn't seem to notice. She was already looking around.

"Must be a jolt," Claire said. "The changes, I mean."

"So many. Even the trees."

"Trees?"

"We had a huge one, right there on the front lawn," Anna said. "A Norway spruce."

"The Derricks," Claire said.

"Who?"

"The people you sold to. The Derricks. We bought the house from them."

"Derricks. Right. I remember."

"They cut it down."

"Loved that tree."

"Guess they wanted an unobstructed view."

"Of what?" Anna said. "Mr. Baughman?"

Claire smiled, stepped back and motioned for Anna to follow.

"Trent said you were in town for some kind of conference?" Claire asked as they headed toward the kitchen.

"Yes. Regional realtors thing, up at the EagleRock Conference Center. Last week it was podiatrists, this week it's realtors."

"And next week it's actuarials," Claire said.

"How'd you know?"

"I'm a speaker at that one."

"Really? You're an actuarial?"

"Statistician," Claire said, stepping into the kitchen. "More like a technical consultant these days, mainly for retailers."

They stopped at the kitchen table. Anna saw the opened laptop and the legal pad.

"Did I disturb your work?"

"Not work. Just a hobby. You want some coffee?"

"No thank you. Coffee'd out," she said as she looked through the kitchen window toward Mr. Baughman's house. He was nowhere in sight.

"Was he here when you were?" Claire asked.

"Hm?"

"Mr. Baughman?"

"Yes. He's just about the only one left from my time. Did some title checks the other night."

"People do move around."

"Hope so. Wouldn't have a job if they didn't," Anna said.

Claire's phone pinged. It was next to the laptop. She didn't reach for it. Anna walked to the center of the kitchen.

"We had an island, right here. Did the Derricks take it out?"

"That was us. It kind of blocked the flow."

"Flow," Anna said. "Well. It feels better, like you can actually *breathe* in here."

"Not when Trent cooks."

They laughed again. Anna looked more relaxed. Claire felt the same. They went to the living room. It was at the back of the house, with a wide picture window looking out over the half-acre backyard. Their property was marked off by a brick wall, with townhouses beyond. Anna lightly clicked her heels on the floor.

"You did it," she said.

"What?"

"Took out the carpeting, exposed the wood."

"Rosewood. Had it sanded and re-varnished."

"We knew it was there," Anna said. "The rosewood. Just never got to it."

Anna kept looking down at the wood. Claire waited. Anna didn't move.

"Time?" Claire asked.

Anna glanced up.

"Sorry?"

"Time," Claire said again. "Did you run out of time?"

"Yes. Time. No time."

Anna walked up to the picture window and looked out.

"Were you here when the townhouses were going up?" Claire asked.

"No. It was wooded," Anna said. She pointed to the center of the yard. "And right there. We had a weeping willow. It was gigantic, really smothered the yard." She turned and looked at Claire.

"Not us. Derricks again."

"I wonder what they had against trees?"

"Maybe they just had a thing for unobstructed views."

Anna smiled. She turned back to the window.

"Under the willow, we had a pond," she said.

"A pond?"

"Not a real pond. More like a hole, lined with concrete," Anna said. "I told your husband about it. We actually kept fish in it."

"No kidding?"

"Carp. Six of them. In the winter we'd bring them inside, keep them in a small aquarium in the basement."

Anna shook her head.

"To think it was once there," she said. "This pond. Our pond, underneath the willow."

Claire heard her phone ping from the kitchen. It was probably Trent, wanting details.

"Still three bedrooms?" Anna asked.

"Yes. No. One's a kind of study now," Claire said as they walked down the hall. She didn't know if she was supposed to feel awkward showing a stranger their master bedroom. She didn't. When they reached the room, Claire stole a reflexive look at the bed to make sure the comforter was properly smoothed, but Anna was looking elsewhere.

"The doors," Ann said. "They're different."

"We replaced them."

"So did I. More than once."

Anne walked up to the bathroom, but didn't go in. She leaned forward for a better look.

"Blue tiles," she said, her voice quavering in the bathroom echo. "Very nice."

She turned and looked at the bathroom door, running her palm along its edge. She said something. Claire couldn't quite hear it.

"What?"

"Deadbolt," Anna said. "I had a deadbolt on mine."

Claire looked at the door. Both went silent. Anna turned to Claire. She didn't seem to blink. Claire felt a sudden need to leave the bedroom. She turned and started back toward the living room. Anna followed. There was another ping from Claire's phone. It was the only sound in the house.

Claire was about to ask if she wanted to see the basement, but Anna stopped at the living room window. She seemed to be looking at the spot where the willow and pond used to be.

"The carp," she said. "Do you want to know what happened to them?"

The phone pinged again. Anna kept looking out the window. Claire didn't answer. She knew she didn't have to.

"We used to go out every other day to, you know, feed them, look in on them," Anna said. "Sometimes the water was so murky you couldn't see them, but you knew they were there. One day in late summer, our last summer here, I want out and they were gone."

Anna stopped, placed her fingertips of her right hand on the glass. She was barely touching it.

"Gone," she said. "The concrete at the bottom of the pond cracked. The water seeped out. Just drained away." She went quiet for a moment. "He was so angry. More than angry. *Furious.*"

Anna turned. Claire saw something like a smile on her face. Not the good kind.

"The thing is, he really didn't care about them. The carp. Ever. I took care of them." She turned and looked out the window again. "His face." She reached up and touched the corner of her right eye, and then put her fingertips back on the glass. "Ok," she said. And then again: "*Ok.*"

They walked back into the kitchen.

"Did you want to see the basement?" Claire asked.

"No. No thank you," Anna said. "Got to go. Conference awaits. I've got a late afternoon seminar."

They walked to the front door. Anna stepped out onto the porch.

"Thank you so much," she said. "And thank your husband."

For what? Claire thought.

"I will," Claire said. "It was very nice meeting you."

Anna smiled, turned and started walking to her car. Claire watched her for a few moments, then looked past her to Mr. Baughman's house. The living room curtains were drawn, but she got the sense someone was watching. Anna got into her car, strapped herself in and waved. Claire waved back, then watched the car go down the street. She closed the door and went back to the kitchen. Her phone pinged, but she didn't touch it. She walked back to the master bedroom. The bathroom light was still on. She went in, turned it off, then wandered back to the living room. She stopped at the window and looked out through the light smudges left by Anna's fingertips. A willow, a pond and carp. Six carp.

I told your husband.

Claire went into the kitchen, opened her laptop, waited for it to boot up, then went to Trent's email portal. Her phone pinged. Claire's fingers tapped at the keys. *SixCarp*. Nothing. She typed in *SixCarpPond*. The emails appeared, tumbling down the screen.

Claire closed her eyes. She wanted a moment before looking. A last moment of peace.

Chris Gates

Emma Bailey Photography

Chris Gates is a Brighton-based writer, actor, director, comic and human man. He has been writing since the age of 13, with a particular focus on short stories over the past couple of years. His greatest influences are Raymond Carver, Max Beerbohm, and Stephen King. *Weaver's Trap* is his first published story.

Weaver's Trap

David was in the kitchen this morning, lurking in the dark as I came down the stairs. He darted to the table as the strip light flickered on. He scraped back my chair and silently gestured for me to sit. I sat. His cold hand brushed against my back, but I didn't flinch. It's amazing what you can get used to.

He made me toast and coffee; I put the radio on because I can't stand the quiet when he's there. I shouldn't have let him do things for me but, in all honesty, I'd started to rely on him; he made me breakfast, he cleaned the bathroom and he ironed my clothes. I couldn't get him to use the vacuum cleaner though. It's the noise, I think.

I sat at the kitchen table, eating my breakfast and trying to forget he was standing behind me. I looked out into the garden in the grey morning light and saw that snow was starting to fall; tiny flakes that melted as soon as they hit the ground. We used to call it suicide snow.

David snatched away my cup and plate as soon as I'd finished and hurried over to the sink to wash up. He craves heat now; hot water, steam from a boiling kettle, hot air from the oven. I once caught him with his face buried in one of my dresses fresh from the tumble dryer. He used to climb into my bed if I got up in the night because he liked to lie in my warm patch. I had to put a stop to that.

My phone rang. I let it ring. I felt him watching over my shoulder as it vibrated on the table; he doesn't like me talking on the phone. He'd smashed five phones in the last year and replacing them was becoming expensive. His hand crept towards it, almost touching my face, but it rang out before he could reach it. His hand slowly withdrew.

Carefully, I picked up the phone and, seeing it was my mother, I stood up and walked calmly towards the back door; he had never liked me talking to her.

The cold pressed painfully against my skin and the patio flagstones were bitter against my bare feet. I shut the door behind me. I took a shivering breath and lifted the phone to my cheek; my mother hadn't spoken to me in a month.

'How's the corpse?' She asked, not even a 'hello'.

'His name's David, Mum.' I said through gritted teeth.

'Fine.' She said, 'how's the corpse you're calling David?'

She's been difficult since she found out; I like to think I would have done something about him before now if only she'd stopped pressuring me. I like to think that.

Still, she kept him a secret and I suppose I should be grateful for that. I sighed down the phone, 'he's the same, Mum.'

'There's someone you should call,' her voice lowered to a whisper 'he's a *freelancer*.'

'How nice for him.' I said.

'Don't be ungrateful!' she spat, 'Do you want it there forever?'

'He won't be here forever,' I said, feeling a small pain grow in my head.

'Really?' She crowed, 'What's going to happen, he can't die again can he?'

Cold air rushed through the gap in my dressing gown and I did nothing to stop it, 'I don't know, Mum.'

'If I give you his number will you call him?'

'You can send me his number.'

'And you'll call him? Today?'

'Just send me the number.'

'Promise me you'll call him.'

'Goodbye Mum.'

I slid my phone into my dressing gown pocket and turned to the door. David's face was pressed up against the window, his hand was on the door handle. We watched each other through the glass as the cold seeped into my bones.

Before getting in the shower I pushed in the lock and moved a chair against the door; he stood outside, as usual, waiting. Afterwards I opened the window to let out all the steam, I waited for my body to cool down before opening the door.

I sat in my towel on the edge of the bath, shivering as the snow fell heavier and heavier.

Leaving the house is sometimes awkward; he follows me down the hall and his body brushes against mine as I try to get out. He was standing very close today, I felt him bump against the front door as I locked it shut. He won't do anything while I'm away, he won't watch television or listen to the radio. He just waits for me to come back home. He's very good at waiting.

I felt my phone pulse in my pocket as I walked to the bus stop, but it was too cold to take off my gloves, so I left it there; I guessed it was just my mother sending me the freelancer's number. I'd heard of such people, of course, and I really couldn't guess how Mum had managed to contact him. I wondered if it was someone from her church.

The heating was broken on the bus to work. I sat with my arms folded in my coat, resting my head against the window and letting the vibrating glass buzz at my skull as the snow and the city blew past.

There was a couple sitting in front of me, both wearing red, her coat and his scarf. The woman was about my age, I think; she was resting her head on his shoulder, he was playing with her hair. Their words were lost under the shuddering diesel engine, but I could hear their voices murmuring; he kept making her laugh, a wild and happy laugh that sirened through the bus, until eventually she punched his shoulder to make him stop talking. I got off a few stops early; I'd be late, but Gaza could open the shop without me.

My shop, mine and Gaza's, Occasional Flowers, hides down a dark, cobblestoned alleyway with black iron lamp posts at either end. Our shop window is a patch of wild colour. We don't get much foot traffic, but business is good; Gaza's husband is in funerals and we do a steady trade with the local parlours. We do weddings as well, though not as many.

Gaza was standing in the doorway when I got there, bundled up in her pink anorak and clumsily holding a cigarette in her mittened hand. She's started smoking again, which is insane at her age. We argued about that for a short while after I stopped, but Gaza won't be told what to do by anyone. She lifted her hood as she heard my footsteps and sang me a good morning. She's been so good to me. She never asks about David and she never pushes. She wants to, though.

I closed the door behind me, shutting her out, and I rushed through the shop down the narrow aisle, making the flowers rustle in their plastic. I saw that Gaza had been working on our commissions; name wreaths spelling out James, Mike, Mum, Dad, Nana. You mainly see these in roses, but we use sunflowers; bright colours make the best funeral flowers.

I was sweeping the floor as Gaza came back inside; a small, graceful woman, like an ancient flamenco dancer with her dramatic black hair and olive skin. She had taken off her bulky anorak and held it folded by her side. She stood beneath the trellis arch by the door, her black dress densely woven with roses; purple, white and blood red blooms. She pressed her painted lips together in a smile and nodded quietly to herself as she watched me avoid her eyes; somehow, I found myself smiling too, as if she and I were sharing a joke.

'Who is Weaver?' She asked, carefully watching my face.

'...Weaver?' I said.

'Yes, darling, Weaver. Don't be shy,' Her smile spread a little more, 'he came in this morning. Weaver, such a pretty name I thought, and he was being very charming, very polite, talking very nice to me, which is always sweet at my age even though he wasn't very handsome, but it was also quite strange, you know, because he seemed to think that he knew me. I thought perhaps that he was just being friendly and was maybe just a little strange; he liked to hear himself talk, I thought, so I started to tell him about the flowers we have, and I showed him the gazanias and made my joke "My name is also Gazania but I am not for sale" and this Mr Weaver, well, when I said that he gave me the Bad Look.' She said, grinning beautifully.

'The bad look?' I said after a moment, because she was clearly waiting for me to ask.

'Yes, darling,' she said, 'the Bad Look. It's the look all men have, even polite and clever men, when they realise that you will not kiss them after the dance. Something goes away in their eyes and suddenly you are not interesting to them anymore, suddenly you are not so pretty. He was very charming still, this Mr Weaver, still so polite, but also somewhere else in his mind... I thought perhaps that he was thinking I was you.' She smiled slyly, 'I told him you might be in later, darling, I hope you do not mind.'

I knew, then. Somehow I just knew.

'And what did he say?' I said quietly.

'Nothing, he just gave me the other look that all men have,' she leaned in and her smile spread wrinkles across her lovely face, 'the one that says "How did Gaza read my mind?"' She laughed again, but briefly; her smile melted as I felt hot blood rush through my body. I grappled for my phone. 'Darling,' Gaza moved quickly towards me, 'you do know this man, don't you? I thought you must have called him for David.'

Hastily, I thumbed open the text message from my mother and my phone shook in my hand as I read it.

Weaver. It said. *All my love. Mum.*

No number. She knew I wouldn't have called him myself.

Suddenly I was screaming. I was screaming and my phone was in pieces on the shop floor and it was so *good* to be angry. I screamed louder. I threw a display of sunflowers to the ground, and threw myself down alongside it, unable to stand, not wanting to stand, wanting to beat my fists against the linoleum and let the pain wash over me. Then I was crying. I hadn't cried in months and my sobs sounded strange, pathetic and weak, and that made me cry harder and that felt good too; the pressure on my throat, the heat in my eyes, the snot running from my nose.

I lay on the floor, curled into a question mark; every sorry thing ripped through my mind and for once I did nothing to stop it and that felt the best of all.

Eventually I lay still, feeling the tears dry to tracks of salt.

Gaza knelt elegantly by my side, smoothing her dress over her legs, her red lips set in a patient line, 'He was here about… your guest, yes?'

'Yes,' I said, my voice weak, 'My mother called him. Apparently he's a freelancer.'

'It was not right of her to call him.' Gaza said, flatly.

'No, it wasn't.'

'But she did call him.'

'Yes, she did.'

'…will you see him?'

I hiccupped and let that stand as a response.

Gaza sighed, 'Darling, get up now,' she helped me into sitting and placed an arm round my shoulders, 'I asked Mr Weaver to wait in the cafe by the station. I said that you would come to see him if you wanted to. If you like, I will go to him now and tell him to leave, to run away and never come back, or perhaps to wait until you are ready. I will do this thing for you, darling,' She said, 'but darling, I think you should go. I think you should go and see him now. I think you must do this thing for yourself.' then Gaza kissed my cheek, pulling me close to her old and graceful frame. I closed my eyes, pressed my face into her neck and breathed in her perfume.

The world revolved around us as she stroked my hair.

It was midnight. Gaza and I were sitting in my kitchen, watching as Weaver assembled his device by the back door, opened out into the night; heavy snowflakes swirled in and settled on his blue overalls.

Years of dealing with funeral men had taught me to expect certain things from professionals who work with death; a kind of practiced reserve, a graveyard manner, a theatrical solemnity as insubstantial as mist drifting over a cemetery. But there was something undeniably solid about Weaver.

Gaza had said he wasn't handsome, which I thought was unfair, though I don't think his looks mattered to him one way or the other. He was a tall man with heavy arms and a jaw that seemed to take up most of his face. He was younger than I expected, clean shaven with a boyish grin, but his black hair was streaked with grey. His eyes were pale and tired.

He had arrived an hour before; I was standing outside shivering in the cold with Gaza while she smoked a cigarette, not wanting to be left inside alone. Weaver approached looking carefully at my neighbour's house he held up a finger to warn us into silence. We stood still, not speaking, but then he nodded briefly to himself and whispered 'hello'. Gaza showed him inside. I lingered on the doorstep, peering in afterwards.

Gaza showed him into the living room where I heard her say 'Mr Weaver, this is David.'

There was a silence. Gaza saw that I had not followed, and she beckoned me forwards, smiling; I took a heavy step inside and slowly pulled the door closed behind me. I joined Gaza by the living room door.

Weaver was approaching David cautiously where he sat in his usual armchair. As I watched, Weaver bent over him, swiftly grabbing his head in both hands; I half stepped towards them, not knowing why.

'Stay nice and still for me please, David', Weaver said, and slipped a hand underneath that cold neck, apparently feeling for a pulse. After a minute had passed, he seemed satisfied that there wasn't one.

He turned to face Gaza and me and smiled 'You can never be too careful,' he said.

Discreetly, Weaver had parked his van in the industrial park around the corner; we walked there together to get his equipment, kept in four heavy backpacks, two of which, the heaviest, he strapped to himself. I carried the other two.

He strolled along the pavement with his hands swinging easily by his sides, his head tilted back, eyes closed against the falling snow as though he were walking in the midday sun.

When we got back, I let Weaver and Gaza go in first. David was still in his armchair, but as we came through, he followed us into the kitchen, walking right behind me, keeping shadow-close like a shy child clinging to its mother. Gaza looked at him, frowning, and suddenly it felt wrong for anyone else to be here. It felt wrong to let anyone else see us together. We had been alone, we had been private, and now here we were. On display.

I set the bag down by the kitchen table and he lurched towards me, reaching out for my face.

'Excuse me,' Weaver murmured, sliding himself between us, once again, grabbing David's head in both hands, forcing it up so that their eyes locked. He slipped both hands down onto David's shoulders and pushed, walking him backwards out of the room, not breaking eye contact.

Gaza came over and put her arms around me. I brushed her off as kindly as I could, wanting to follow Weaver into the other room, but he was already coming back into the kitchen. He calmly closed the kitchen door, holding it shut, motioning for me to push the kitchen table up against it. 'Better to keep David out of the way.' He said and smiled.

'Is he okay?' I said without thinking.

Weaver nodded, kindly touching my arm.

He asked me to turn off the heating, he said that Gaza and I should keep on our winter gear and make some tea, then he unpacked his equipment and began to build. We all started breathing mist as cold crept through the house.

After a while, we heard a noise at the kitchen door. A scratching on the wood. Weaver paused briefly, checking that the table was hard up against the door before turning back to his work.

When we had spoken earlier in the café by the station, Weaver had talked of using a 'Heat Trap,' and the image that popped into my head was something like a large toaster, but as he worked and it began to take shape, I saw that it looked more like a coffin.

When he lifted it onto its end, it stood about six feet tall, a white metal shell with a black handle, and a gondola stencilled in red on the front. Weaver clearly wanted me to ask about the stencil, but I wasn't in the mood to indulge him. He plugged it in to a socket on the wall and, from inside, we heard something start to hum.

'We've just got to let her warm up,' he said, and started to gather together his bags.

The scratching came at the door again.

'He can feel us in here,' Weaver said quietly, 'but he won't get in until I move the table, and I won't move the table until the Heat Trap is ready.' He turned to Gaza and me, and whispered, 'you should both wait outside,' he said, 'he should go straight for the trap, it'll be the warmest thing in the room, but there's no need to take chances.'

'But what about you, Mr Weaver?' Gaza said, 'What happens to you?'

'I'll be fine, Miss Gaza' he said, and winked 'I'm cold blooded.'

The snow had slowed and the clouds overhead had thinned, showing

Gaza and I the full moon. Our shadows were like puddles of ink on the patio.

Our arms were linked, Gaza was smoking another cigarette. We could see Weaver through the window, sitting on the table in front of the kitchen door, occasionally he looked at his watch.

I felt a weight pressing on my stomach and, without meaning to, I made a sound in my throat; Gaza looked over and kissed me gently, blowing either smoke or mist in my face, 'Don't worry darling,' she said, 'this is a hard thing for you, yes? But it is the right thing, it is. You must know that.'

I shook my head, 'None of this was supposed to happen, Gaza,' I said, wearily, 'so I don't know if this is the right thing to do. It's just what I'm doing.'

I sighed. Weaver waited. Gaza smoked.

'Can I have a cigarette please?' I said, and even though she gave me a hard look she didn't argue. It had been a year. She passed one over, along with her own to light it. It tasted awful, just awful, but after a few drags I felt the nicotine tingling under my skin. I felt dizzy with it, I rested my head against Gaza's shoulder.

Inside, Weaver hopped off the table. He walked over to the Heat Trap, pressing a hand against the door before heaving it open; a dark red glow filled the kitchen. We could feel the heat bleeding through into the night. Through the window I watched Weaver heave the table to one side.

The kitchen door banged open and my cigarette fell forgotten to the floor.

Radhika Kapur

Radhika Kapur's work as a copywriter has won awards at Cannes, One Show, Clio and Asia Pacific Adfest. She was longlisted for BBC's Drama Scriptroom in 2017, the London Short Story Prize in 2016 and won third place in the Euroscript Screenwriting Competition in 2015. Her short fiction has been published by literary journals and in the anthologies: *Love Across a Broken Map* and *May We Borrow Your Country*. Radhika is a member of the South Asian Writers' Collective, The Whole Kahani, and has completed an MA in Screenwriting from Birkbeck College, University of London.

The School Play

'Don't you know Gandhiji was vegetarian? I can't eat biryani,' Saeed crossed his hands across his chest, sat at the dining table. He lifted his chin and looked determinedly away from the biryani, staring at the Maggi Hot & Sweet Sauce, next to stainless steel spoons crowding the chipped metal spoon holder, instead. 'But you're not really Gandhiji, it's just a role in a play that the teacher has given you' quipped Sameena, her eyes sparkling with five-year-old life, her pigtails swinging with it, 'So you can.' His mother, a woman with a harried look stamped on her face, no matter how she arranged it, rolled her eyes, 'Well there's nothing else made. So are you going on hunger strike then?' 'Yes! Hunger strike!' Saeed shouted lifting a spoon high in the air. His fervour made up for its washed-out steel dullness. Until the aroma of succulent, saffron flavoured mutton wafted past. The mutton peeped through the rice, tempting him, just like his best friend, Raghav's face in the window, calling him to play cricket. Oh he couldn't look away. 'Ok, maybe I will eat it this time. So that you don't feel bad. But, please don't make any more non-veg till the Independence Day function is over.' 'Right, because I don't feel bad. What happened to your hunger strike?' asked his mother, heaping a spoonful of rice on his plate. 'The

British have already gone. What will I go on hunger strike for,' he shot back with a grin.

The next day, Saeed stared at the empty auditorium and banged an imaginary staff into the stage floor, 'Do or die!' 'Do or die' chorused a bunch of eleven-year-olds behind him in shrill, unbroken voices as they practiced for their performance. Raghav put his finger up his nose and extracted a long bogey as he shouted out the slogan. Their voices were dwarfed by the vast, empty space, sucked in by the dusty floor and trapped in the stacked chairs leaning indolently against the wall. Miss Barua, their drama teacher, watched them out of her hawk eyes, sitting on one of the folding metal chairs in the front. Rumour had it that the big red bindi on her forehand was her third eye. Its scrutiny reached out of its maroon sun, searing Saeed. She was a formidable force and when she walked even her sari shrank away from her feet. 'More energy! Are you fighting for your country or reading out the electricity bill,' she boomed. Saeed scraped some extra volume off the sides of his throat as he shouted, 'Do or die!' Raghav muttered 'Poop or cry,' under his breath. Saeed smothered a giggle and it tickled his throat mercilessly.

It became Raghav's battle cry. He hid behind the grand, white pillar near the girl's toilet during the afternoon break. 'Poop or cry, poop or cry' he screamed every time a girl entered or left the toilet. His peals of laughter multiplied like numbers under the high-ceilinged corridor. Raghav wasn't scared of anything, not even his mother. In fact, it was the other way round. Saeed could see it in her quivering lip and blinking eyes when she came to pick Raghav up from the bus stop, as if asking, but not daring to ask, what did you do today? Rolling the unasked question into tight little balls and stuffing them into her ears so she wouldn't hear the answer. Raghav's mother looked like she must be scared of many things, like cockroaches, darkness and cracked frames.

There was a cracked frame in the school corridor they were standing in. Inside it was a picture of Maulana Abul Kalam Azad, the freedom fighter and the first education minister of India. It was a frame that had been cracked by a cricket ball that had been aimed at it purposefully. It's because the Maulana was Muslim. That's what everyone said. The high ceiling was a mathematician. It could multiply anything. Laughter, shrieks, and unnamed feelings that crawl around the corners of a body like a cockroach.

Two girls from a senior class sashayed out, skirt hems higher than they were supposed to be. Raghav jumped right in their path. 'Poop or cry!' They screamed and jumped back. 'Stupid fool' one of them yelled as Raghav parroted, 'Stupid fool!' Saeed sniggered, still safely behind the pillar.

Later that night, Saeed sat cross-legged on the tiled floor of his bedroom, as he took out his pencils from his military tank pencil box that his uncle had got him from Dubai. They clattered, rolling on the floor, sharpened pointy pencils, a collection of missiles, raring to win wars and conquer brown-paper-covered schoolbooks. Then his homework-melted eraser and dinky car. He carefully transferred them to his old case. He picked up the soft plastic tank and smelt it. It still had the new smell. No trace of battles with the tiffin box inside the school bag. The fan hummed softly overhead, lifting the soft hair at his nape. A whiff of the Queen of the Night had him closing his eyes and inhaling. In the black space behind his eyelids, he scrawled 'No foreign goods' with an imaginary green, glitter pen. At least, not till Independence Day, still a week away, an eternity stretching into the future like an infinite, cosmic bubble gum.

'You can have it,' he handed the tank pencil case to Raghav, the next morning, perched under the banyan tree in the school courtyard. Raghav's eyes were wide, in fact in danger of dropping off and turning into marbles if they dilated any more. For a moment the image occupied Saeed completely. Raghav eyeless, schoolchildren playing marbles with his eyeballs. 'Are you serious,' clamoured Raghav, 'No wait, do you want something in return, something really big?'

'You can give it back to me after Independence Day'

'What? Why?'

'Till then I am Gandhiji and I'm only using things made in India.'

'But you should continue being him, even after,' exclaimed Raghav examining the tank from every angle.

Saeed knew that but it felt too difficult. Guilt rose up in him now that Raghav had pressed him to make eye contact with it. 'Ok you can have it for two days, even after the function,' Saeed said in order to appease that wagging finger inside his head. Saeed thought of the black and white diagram of the mayfly in his Science book that lived its whole life in 24 hours. Two days was two lifetimes.

Raghav whipped the case away before Saeed could change his mind. His blue shirt stuck to his body and the wet patches under his arm-pits bulged as he clasped it to his chest. 'Ok now that you've given me this, I'll tell you a secret.' He looked around, carefully cataloguing the crow picking at tiffin crumbs at their feet, the bangle-pink bougainvillea clambering up the wall and Don, the bulky seventeen-year old basketball captain, dribbling a basketball, on the court across from them. Raghav lowered his voice, 'Don asked how come they've made you Gandhi in the play, when we have so many Hindus around.' Suddenly, a warm gust blew dust into their eyes. God sweeping the heavens, his mother would say. A swinging root of the banyan tree swayed, entangling Saeed's small hands, trying to swat the dust away. He jumped off the cement seat around the tree. Don was the boy who cracked the frame in the corridor. Saeed looked towards the basketball court furtively. Don jumped up and threw the ball. His still chubby flesh undulated. The ball arced into the basket perfectly, then fell to the ground with a thud. He let out a triumphant grunt. An adoring junior ran to pick the ball up. He held it out like an offering. Don had amassed a band of followers by displaying his prowess in winning fights with his fists, especially after inter-school matches with members of the opposing team.

'What did you say?'

I said, 'I never thought of him as Hindu.'

'Neither did I.'

Saeed couldn't imagine Gandhiji having a religion. He thought he was a religion. So many people followed him – just like Prophet Muhammad, Krishna or Jesus. The idea of him following a religion made him seem small and ordinary, suddenly. A significant step down from morning assembly prayer status.

At home, Saeed scrawled his homework into his book diligently, sitting at the dining table. Today's task was to guess the synonym:

Eraser – rubber.

Small – little.

The matter of Gandhiji being Hindu continued to preoccupy him. After all, he did say 'Hey Ram' when the bullet went through him.

What was the synonym for Ram?

Allah…?

He stared at his notebook, pencil hovering above the page.

'What's the matter?' his mother asked. The TV news blared in the background. A man shouted, 'If you think India isn't tolerant, go to Pakistan!' Words like steel glasses, falling one on top of the other. A deafening crashing of metal against metal. 'A boy asked why they have made me Gandhiji, when there are so many Hindus around.' His mother squinted her eyes and snorted. There was an out-of-order washing machine in the living room. It had been heaved and pushed in there by determined hands and floral-nightie covered hips, just until they got rid of it. It was still there. There was a doily on top of it now, with a vase bursting with artificial flowers. It even got dusted everyday. She looked at it and the thought that prejudice had become like furniture and washing machines that masqueraded as furniture – a part of life, for her. 'What an uneducated comment. Tell them he was an Indian first,' she said dismissing it.

Was Gandhi Hindu or Indian first? Who decides what comes first? Saeed lay awake, staring at the shapes of light and shadow on the ceiling. A car rumbled into silence in the distance. He always came first in class. His marks decided that. Marks are easy. Surely being Indian carries more marks than being Hindu, he thought. A peace descended on him, softer than the muslin sheet covering his body.

The day had finally come. He felt as excited as he felt on his birthday or Eid. The clock ticked slowly unwrapping the hours. The school bus sputtered down the busy street. Traffic fumes wiggled into his nostrils and he pressed his nose harder against the window to keep them out. The hazy air, the blurry city were an hourglass catapulting him back in time. Hurrying pedestrians turned into young men waving the Indian flag, chanting Inqilab Zindabad. Banging hearts bursting through skin. Perhaps this is how it felt in the hours before 15th August, 1947, thought Saeed. The anticipation so sharp, it was painful.

The skin-coloured cap was like a swimming cap, only thinner. It hid Saeed's hair and made him appear bald. It stretched over his head rubbery-tight. Like jars that don't open, secrets behind lips and stubborn tooth paste at the end of a rolled-up tube. The make-up aunty brushed his skin with swirls of powder. She told Saeed about the TV actors' faces she transforms. The white elastic dhoti fluttered every time the pedestal fan turned their way. A pair of wire-frame round specs weighed down his ears. He looked in the mirror. He saw Mohandas Karamchand Gandhi stare back.

His shoulder blades jolted. An overpowering emotion rose up in him. India love. It sang through his nails, rippled across his back and swum out of his trembling knees. It was like loving someone you've always loved, for the first time. Saeed couldn't remember when he understood that he loved his mother, it felt like knowledge he was born with, but surely there must have been a moment and it must have been as giddy as this. Before he knew it, it was time for them to go on stage and Mrs Barua was sweeping them towards it.

The velvet curtains rose up. The freedom fighters marched across the stage chanting, 'Do or die' as a packed auditorium watched in hollowed-out darkness. Saeed led the band of mini men and women, his voice ablaze, the tricolour held high. Sparks of light flew off him. Beads of pride adorned his mother's chest. Sameena's fidgeting stilled. Her eyes widened. Flood lights watched and curtains on the stage sides didn't twitch once.

Costume and makeup intact, Saeed and Raghav sprinted out of the greenroom into a narrow pathway, flanked by brick walls on either side. Mango trees rose up behind it and their feet gobbled their long shadows.

'Do or cry!'

'Poop or die!'

'Do or cry!'

'Poop or die!'

'Do or cry!'

'Poop or die!'

'Do or – '

Saeed banged into a hard wall and stumbled, dust flying under his skidding feet. He looked up. It was the frame cracker – Don, a cigarette he wasn't supposed to be smoking, dangling from his chubby fingers. He scratched his nose, rubbing the ridge of it up and down and looked at Saeed like a specimen under the microscope.

'Oh the Muslim. I can't understand how they could make you Gandhi?'

Saeed was brave today. Braver than he had ever been.

'What's Hindu or Muslim got to do with it?'

'Because all Muslims are Pakistani and that's where you belong.'

'That's a really uneducated comment, ' Saeed said echoing his mother.

Don flushed a warm-blooded red. Raghav's head swivelled towards Saeed, his eyes tinged with surprise and flecks of fear. Don spat the cigarette out of his mouth. Its orange embers landed on maroon gravel, warning it. He looked at a point behind them. There were some boys watching curiously at the entrance to the greenroom. The air seemed to hold its breath.

'Hey who wants to play Partition-Partition?'

Their eyes lit up, hands shot up.

'We do' they clamoured.

'Well then, during Partition Hindus beat up Muslims, so 1, 2… 3'

The boys rushed towards Saeed. The air exhaled, and the long leaves on the trees danced and rustled, like a peacock's feathers. Green mangoes on curved branches bobbed gently.

Saeed stepped back. Sneakers slamming grit got closer and closer. His ragged breath, louder. Rumbling traffic faded. Suddenly they were all around him. The boys giggled and kicked and giggled. Sweet, high-pitched angelic giggles.

'Let's send him to Pakistan! Let's send him to Pakistan!'

Raghav shoved one of them.

'Leave him alone!'

Don's hand landed across his shoulder, pinning him in place.

'Pakistani! Pakistani,' he chanted.

One voice turned into a flower bunch of voices.

Saeed fell to the ground, his thigh burned. Gravel went everywhere. The white dhoti, turned rusty. He hooked his hand around a boy's leg and tugged. The boy fell with a thud. All the while a silent-loud voice inside whispered 'Slap slap, other cheek'. A smelly sneaker stamped his face. Another crushed the round wire-frame spectacles, melting its shape. A foot slammed into his stomach. Such was its force, it must have gone through and be sticking out of his back. 'Should we take his dhoti off,' asked one.

'No no, that's being mean,' answered another.

'Oh then let's not.'

Adult voices rounded the corner. Suddenly, Don slunk away. Raghav bolted forward, barreling into a body. One of the boys fell. He scrambled up. They turned and ran. Raghav ran trembling fingers through his hair and spit out a defiant laugh, 'Saw how they ran…' A mango fell at his feet with a thud. He jumped. Suddenly, he burst into heaving tears, 'Mummy,' he snivelled and sobbed, nose bulbous and red. His eyes wrung every drop out of his knotted insides.

Saeed, bald and skinny, in a white dhoti, lay panting, eyes shut, long eyelashes fanning his face. They lifted up slowly, 'Hey Ram, don't cry so loudly,' he said.

Barbara Leahy

Barbara Leahy is from Cork, Ireland. Her short stories have appeared in literary magazines and anthologies including *Flash* magazine, *The Irish Literary Review*, and the *Bridport Prize Anthology*, and have been broadcast on RTÉ (Irish National) radio. She is a past winner of the Wells Festival of Literature Short Story Competition, and the Words With Jam Shortest Story Competition. Earlier this year, she was shortlisted for the Edinburgh International Flash Fiction Award.

The Time It Takes to Smoke a Cigarette

I expected the first winter in the north-west to kill me but it turned out milder than promised. By February, melting snow was dripping from the cabin roof and dropping in soft drifts from the pines. The blue grass rustled with garter snakes and grasshoppers, and every living thing looked like it had woken from a long and mellow sleep. No greater mishaps had befallen me than a few trees blocking the road from time to time, and that kind of mishap suits me fine. It's not much of a road, just a dirt track that rambles down the mountain and doesn't meet asphalt until the town is in sight. I take the pick-up down once a month if the road's passable, and I go to the bank to check the money's still coming, and to buy whatever I need. I talk to nobody, and nobody talks to me.

The day I signed for the cabin, I went to meet the owner in town, at a diner where the air-conditioning was broken and the swampy heat of summer seeped through the walls. His fleshy hand gripped mine in a damp greeting. Even at arm's length, he smelled of cooking fat and coffee. Flies sought out the crevices of his face and he smacked and rubbed at them as though trying to work them into his skin.

'Gotta husband? he asked. 'Kids?' His tongue worried something stuck in his teeth.

I busied myself with the envelope, counted six months' rent onto the table.

He looked at the dollars, at me: at my faded shirt, my long greying hair twisted into a bandana, my work-rough hands.

'No place for a lady on her own,' he said, but he took my money anyway. Once, in the early days, he came up here. To check on me.

'Dogs don't like visitors,' I told him, after I'd called them off.

Up here there's no electricity, no phone, no people. You've got to park up and tramp through sagebrush to get to the clearing beyond the cedars where the cabin stands. It's a basic construction: a wooden shack raised on slats with a pitched roof. Out front is a rotting porch with a low roof where mosquitoes gather. Out back is a clearing with a lot of old tree stumps like someone planned on building something here but thought better of it. Around the stumps, the scrub's scabby with burnt growth, and there's a scattering of rusted twists of metal. A river runs fast behind the cabin, and, from mid-stream, I can see down to the valley, where tree-tops shuffle like the earth's quaking beneath them. The quiet up here is supposed to bring peace but it brings watchfulness too. Some days the silence makes me creep around like I'm waiting for a hand to fall on my shoulder. On those nights I lie, shivering with gratitude, listening to the coyotes howl. These past few days, dry heat is in my bones, in my head. One spark could set everything alight.

Today was hot enough to kill my oldest dog, a blind and stubborn stray I'd found wandering in the woods. I leave the corpse on a bed of knapweed and go to the river to cool down, wading out and standing up to my neck in rushing water, and when I feel my heart beating nice and slow, I get out, pull on my jeans and shirt over my wet skin and pick up the shovel. I'm not sentimental, but I find myself whispering words of remorse to that sweet old boy as I dig the hole. Soft green spiders hide in froth on blades of grass, as though a fizz of white bubbles can protect them, and I wonder if I'll ever be safe to go back home. I lie my no-name dog in a shady copse among bluebells and wild garlic, a place that's all kinds of lovely if you notice that sort of thing, and when I finish, I look up to see the tall grass warp and weave around a stranger approaching in the distance.

A man. Nearly always a man. Not many make it this far, and if they do, they've got a reason.

This one says he's looking for his daughter.

'There was trouble,' he says, pulling off a battered cowboy hat.

His voice rolls round his mouth like gravel. Fifty, or thereabouts, and not long on the road. More lean than thin; nothing spare. The type who'd kill a buffalo, eat his fill, then cure the hide and boil the hooves and twist fishing line from the guts. A few days' growth on his tanned face and no more dirt than you'd gather in a couple of nights rough. Washed-out jeans and old hiking boots. A backpack drops to his feet like an anchor.

'Lots of trouble around, these days,' I say. There's nothing but me between him and my door and I think of my axe and how quickly I can get to it. I pick up the shovel and stake the blade in the earth between us.

'I hate to impose,' he says, raising his brows, and his brown eyes narrow at the corners where his brown skin creases, and he's looking at me all wistful earnestness. I see how this is meant to play, and I wonder how much he knows about me. Sticking out of his pocket is the hilt of a knife he's careful to let me see.

Better to invite him in than turn him away with a grudge.

Inside is darker than it should be. One filmy window lets in meagre light and little air. Some long-gone dweller's staleness lingers, and no sunshine, wind, or rain ever clears it. There are two rooms, one big, one small, which is one more than I need. Alongside the door's a row of nails where I hang anything that can be hung. A stove sits on loose slates, a pile of chopped birch beside it. On a counter made of fruit crates stands a stoneware jug, a ladle, a knife, a fork, a plate and some mugs. There's a hand-sawn table, a couple of chairs rough with splinters, some cupboards to keep provisions off the beetle-infested floor, and that's it. Overhead, there's a shelf under the rafters where I climb up to sleep the rare times I've got company, pulling the ladder up after me. Mostly, I make my bed right here by the stove. I set the man at one end of the table, light the tinder, and open a can of stew.

'Only picture I got is one her mother sent years ago.' He flattens a tattered photograph onto the table and I take a look. A child with long red hair, holding a dead fox by its hind legs. He pins down the curling edges with dirty fingertips. Trouble's grained into his skin, slicked under his nails.

'Course she looks a little older now. Only got to know her this past year, and now she's gone,' he says.

'Better get your searching done before dark,' I say.

The stew's bubbling on the stove.

'She's smart,' he says. 'And tough. I seen her skin a goat in the time it takes to smoke a cigarette.'

I bring a plate of food and two mugs of coffee and sit down. You can tell a lot about a man by the way he eats. This one leans into the plate like someone's going to snatch it away and he delivers each forkful as fast as he can swallow. He smacks his lips, wipes his tongue across his brown teeth. When he drinks, he throws his head back, his Adam's apple bobs, and he reminds me of a snake swallowing some small creature. The mug comes down with a thud, the coffee all drunk up.

Out come a tobacco pouch and papers.

'Smoke?'

'Only on special occasions,' I say, and he laughs.

'I heard about you down town,' he says, rolling a cigarette. The long, stained fingers are surprisingly nimble. He licks the paper, seals it, slides his chair nearer to reach the stove. First I smell meat on his breath, then smoke. In his eyes are darts of sickly yellow. I'm close enough to part the tiny forking lines at their corners. I wonder how the jagged tips of his teeth would feel under my tongue.

'I heard you were crazy to find some place where you'd be all alone. Now that's not social behaviour, living up here away from folks, turning your dogs on anyone comes calling.'

He smiles his brown-toothed smile. 'I reckon you got trouble, just like me.'

I've seen that smile before, I know its polite menace and what it hides: the lust for fear and panic; the need for some swift and foolish act.

I slide my hand across the table towards him. In one movement, I crumple the picture of the girl, toss her into the stove. She flares and blackens, leaves a sour smell.

'Search all you want but you won't find her, not a hair, not a tooth, not a fingernail,' I say. 'I caught that little bitch breaking in here one night, so I took that axe you see over the door and swung it wide and cracked her skull. Felled her. She lay bleeding on the floor, round about where you laid your backpack.'

I look right into his speckled eyes. 'She died in the time it took to smoke a cigarette.'

He takes in a great breath, and for a second I think of the knife and how it might feel against my neck, and then he laughs, a gut-laugh. He stands up and laughs so hard I think he's going to be sick all over the floor. I won't need my shelf under the rafters tonight, won't need to hoist the ladder up after me, because he's gathering up his tobacco, his hat; he's hefting the backpack up on his shoulders and now he's out the door, crossing the porch, still laughing. I stand in the doorway and watch him pass the thicket with its fresh wild grave, watch him kick his way through the undergrowth until the long grass closes behind him. I listen to him whistling his way back to the track. Then I go inside, and stir the ashes in the stove.

Michael Mau

Michael Mau is a writer, teacher, actor, artist, and snappy dresser. Michael's short fiction has appeared in *Black Warrior Review*, *New Limestone Review*, *Portland Review*, and other places. *An Open Letter to America From a Public School Teacher*, originally published in *McSweeney's*, received national attention when it was picked up by several news outlets. His story *Little Bird* was selected by Lily Hoang as the winner of the *Black Warrior Review Fiction Contest*. Michael was a finalist for the 2017 and 2018 Disquiet Prize. Visit him at www.michaelmau.org or on Instagram

Pal

I lay on the floor in the darkness of the living room, a thin layer of curtain protecting me from the eyes of the man and lady who were looking through the window by the front door. Knocking, they peered in one at a time. Halos of sunlight crowned their heads. If I didn't move, they wouldn't see me, and they would think no one was home, and they would leave.

They weren't leaving though, and the longer they stood there, the greater the chance that Pal would make a noise, and they would know we were home, and they would take him away.

I crawled across the floor toward the hall.

"Kid," Pal called from our room.

A shadow in the window told me they had heard him.

"Kid," he yelled louder.

The knocking again.

"Mrs. Franklin," said the woman.

"Peeeee," yelled Pal. "Uh oh."

I got up and ran to quiet Pal. The back door opened; a man called out, "Mrs. Franklin."

"Evander, this is Pal," I say.

Pal repeats his name, only it sounds like he is calling for himself on the other side of the house. Because he can't extend his arm, Pal sticks out his elbow. The eczema is back. I'll have to get cream when I buy diapers.

"Evander," says Evander, and reaches down for Pal's elbow.

Pal shouts Evander's name – only it sounds more like Ender – jabs his elbow in Evander's direction.

"You do like this," I say and touch the tip of my elbow to the tip of Pal's. "It's called a noop."

"Nooooop!" Pal calls out as if he is cheering on his favorite basketball player. He bounces in his chair.

I can see that Evander is scared, so I tell Pal we are going to go hang out in our room.

"Room," Pal announces.

Walking down the hall, Evander looks at all of the photos. Most are of me as a baby, but there is one of Mom and Pal sitting on the back of her motorcycle.

"Is that your mom?" he asks.

"Mom," Pal repeats from the next room. He is letting me know that he is still paying attention – that he is a responsible parent.

"No, that's Pal," I say. "The other one's my mom. Come on." My funny way of avoiding a conversation about her.

Mom is out there in the world somewhere, free from me and Pal.

"Come on," Pal says.

When Pal had called out, he wasn't telling me he had to pee. He was telling me he had peed. From the trail and the puddles, I knew he had tried to get out of bed himself and get into his wheelchair.

"Oh, Pal," I said to him, mostly out of disappointment in myself for not waking him up and making him pee.

"Oh, Kid," he said. Our own call and response.

"Pal, we have to –"

"Man!" yelled Pal, sitting half in his wheelchair.

"What is going on here?" the man asked. "Where is your mother?"

The woman was right behind him, eyes wide, hand gripping the man's shoulder. "That man has no pants on."

She pushed past the man and moved to take my arm. I fell back into Pal's lap, and my weight pushed the wheelchair back, sending both of us to the floor.

"Fuck you," yelled Pal, holding me as best he could with both of his arms, his legs twisted and kicking.

I usher Evander into our room.

As soon as he crosses the threshold, Evander covers his nose and mouth. "It smells like pee."

"Pee," shouts Pal, and I can hear him bouncing in his chair. He thinks this is funny.

"It's the mattress," I say. "I wash the sheets when he pees, but really the only thing you can do with the mattress is put it out in the sun. You get used to it. Check this out." I point to the wall of shelves displaying Pal's models.

Ever since he was little, Pal had been building models. At first, he would just buy the kits and put them together. That got boring, he said, so he built what he called "custom jobs." I call them Frankencars. My favorite is a purple truck that looked like the car from The Munsters, but it was also a limousine. I named it Grapico after my favorite soda. Pal had told me that it took five different model kits to create it.

I am explaining this to Evander when he reaches for Grapico.

"No," I yell, batting his hand away. "Don't touch."

"Touch," comes Pal's voice from the living room.

"Sorry," I tell Evander as I stand between him and the shelves. "We don't touch them. They're just for looking." And then, "Hey, look at this one. Pal built the engine out of the plastic trees. They're also called runners or grids. Pal told me –"

"How can he even –" Evander starts to ask, but I know where he's going.

"He built them before he crashed Mom's motorcycle. That's why we don't touch. He can't do it anymore."

"I think I need to go," says Evander, backing away towards the bed, but then he avoids the bed and backs towards the window.

"Wait," I plead. I know that if Evander leaves, I will have no friends. "Have you ever shot a gun?" I ask, moving to the closet to retrieve Pal's air rifle. "It's not a real gun," I say. "Well, it's real, but..." I hold it out for Evander to take. "You can hold it."

Unlike with the models that he was so eager to put his hands on, Evander is less enthusiastic about the gun.

"Do I need to call the police?" the man asked.

The woman wasn't listening. "Sir," she said. "You have to let go." And then to me: "Selena, where is your mother? We need to –"

"Fuck you," I said. Normally, I wouldn't say things like that, but Pal had said it, so I thought it would be okay. It wasn't.

"Noooo," said Pal, chastising me for my language.

"Call them," the lady said. "And tell them they'll need to bring a van."

They were going to take him. I knew for sure. I could see it all: the police wheeling him into a van, Pal in an orange jumpsuit, me talking to him on a phone behind a thick window. I couldn't not cry.

The man was on the phone, the woman was crouching next to us, I was sobbing, and Pal loosened his grip. Maybe he didn't have the strength to hold me; maybe he got one of his bad cramps; maybe he knew it was inevitable.

The lady took me by the arm and led me into the living room. My pajama pants were soaked through with Pal's pee.

"We'll go into the backyard and set up some milk jugs," I say to Evander.

He softens and maybe even brightens up, but this doesn't last.

"Uh oh. Uh oh. Uh. Oh," yells Pal.

He has had an accident.

I leave the gun with Evander and go to check on Pal.

He has diarrhea. It's not a bunch, but I don't want him to get a rash because little rashes turn into big rashes and big rashes bust open and bleed and get this sticky white stuff. Then Pal can't sit in his chair, which means he can't get around the house, which means I have to stay home from school. I like school, and Pal wants me to go to school. So I need to change Pal.

I call back to Evander to help me.

He walks into the room, rifle in hand like he needs to protect me.

"Put the gun down," I say. "You just have to get Pal's pants at the ankles and pull so I can hold Pal."

I usually have to do it myself, so having Evander here is a big help. Only Evander doesn't want to help. "It's not a big deal," I tell him. "You won't get any of it on you." He looks like he's going to cry, so I tell him it's okay. Pal has a mess all over him. It's in his hair, which is always hard to get out. I'll have to give him a bath, but for now I can use wet wipes. "Can you at least get the wet wipes from the bathroom," I tell Evander, and he does.

"Scared, "says Pal.

"Why are you scared?" I ask.

"Boy," says Pal.

"You don't need to be scared of him," I tell him. "You need to be scared of tomato soup, Pal."

"Boy scared," says Pal.

He's worried about Evander.

"Selena," the lady asked, "who is that man?"

"Who are you?" I sassed back to her.

"My name is Linda Sears; I'm with the cabinet for families and children. Mr. Byers and I are here to help you. Now, who did you say that man was? He can't be your father."

My father had died when I was two or three, and the lady must have known that. I didn't know whether to say he was my stepdad, or my mom's boyfriend, or what, so I said, "That's Pal. We take care of each other."

I didn't know to say that Pal had been my dad's best friend, and when Dad died, Pal and my mom became like my mom and my dad. I didn't want to tell her that the year before, they rode home from a bar on Mom's motorcycle, and they crashed. Mom broke her arm, but Pal hit his head. Maybe Mom had hit her head, too, because she got really angry all the time. She would call Pal a retard and tell him that she was just going to take off. Then she did. She left Pal; and she left me. Pal and I had to take care of each other, because we were all we had.

"Kid," Pal called from the bedroom. "Kid."

"What are you going to do?" I asked the lady.

"Oh, Selena," she said, looking at me like I was some puppy.

That's when the police showed up.

Evander comes back with Clorox wipes, and I have to go get the wet wipes myself.

"Alright, little baby, it's time for your bath," I say to Pal.

It's a joke we have, and he usually laughs, but today he says, "No."

It's because Evander is here, and Pal is embarrassed.

Pal's pants go by the backdoor. I'll have to use the hose on them first. I just dump the diaper out there, too. Evander looks more like he's watching a scary movie than watching someone get changed. He has a little brother, so I know he's seen this before. I have to hold Pal's penis and testicles to get underneath, which is actually a lot easier to clean than the harrier parts. The clean-up isn't as bad as I expected. I only use six wipes. It's not perfect, but he's clean enough. Only because we have company, I forgot to get the new diaper, so I have to leave Pal and Evander together. "I have to get a diaper," I tell Evander. "You'll be okay." You have to do that with kids sometimes — remind them that they're fine.

"Everything's going to be fine," the lady said as she opened the door for the policemen. "They're in the back room," she told them.

"Don't hurt him," I told the men.

"Where is your mother?" the lady asked again. "Is she at work?"

"She doesn't live here," I said. "It's just me and Pal."

"And Pal —" but the yelling from the bedroom stopped her.

I could hear men saying things like, "Sir, we just need to — ," and "If you'll just calm down." Pal was yelling at them, but it didn't sound like Pal.

One of the policemen came in and told the lady, "We are going to move him, so you may want to —" he made a sweeping gesture with his hand to tell her she needed to get rid of me.

"Let's go for a walk, Selena," she said, leading me toward the kitchen.

"The diapers are in the bathroom," I said to the policeman. It was the only thing I had any control over, and I didn't want Pal to go to jail naked.

I bring back his diaper and some powder. There's only one left, so we'll have to go to the store later. I was going to get pants, but I know that as soon as Evander leaves, it's bath time for Pal. I don't even ask Evander for help rolling Pal off the towel. Pal's pretty good at doing that himself anyway. The towel goes out with the pants and old diaper. I am an expert at diapering. Lift, slide, strap, stick, strap, stick, done. Pal drags himself over to the couch. As he gets close to Evander, Evander backs into the coffee table and about breaks his leg. I don't say anything or help him back up. Pal can get himself up on the couch, but I help him anyway. I wish that Evander hadn't come over. I like him, still, but he makes me feel bad about Pal. And Pal doesn't like it when I feel bad about him.

Pal was yelling for me – "Kid, Kid, Kid" – but the lady was pushing me out the back door, telling me it would be okay. She kept calling me "Selena," which no one ever called me except teachers on the first day of school.

There was a crashing sound in the house, and I imagined the shelves of Pal's model cars smashed and destroyed on the floor. "Please, sir," I heard a man say.

I wanted to run to Pal, to grab anything I could from the kitchen and fight the men off. I would hit them, and Pal would kick them when they were down. We'd escape and start over somewhere else.

Living with Pal had taught me not to be scared. Before the accident, Pal would tell me, "No fear, Kid." He even had a shirt that said that. Afterwards, when Pal was in his chair and he couldn't do things anymore, Mom had gotten really angry. She'd yell at Pal, and she'd yell at me, and she'd stay out all night.

When she hadn't come home for a week, and I was crying and

confused, Pal had wheeled himself over to the couch where I was sleeping, and tried to tell me, "No Fear." It had sounded like, "Near." We hadn't done all of our talking practice yet.

Hearing Pal calling out and hearing the crash, I was right back to being eight. I closed my eyes and repeated "Near" over and over until the lady said, "Does anyone live here except you and that man?"

"I have to go," Evander says. "I have to go."

"Go," says Pal, nodding his head. "Go home. Home. Go."

Evander stands there like he's waiting for me to open the door for him. "Go then," I say, and I feel terrible because I sound like Mom. I soften and tell him, "I'll see you at school."

"Boy," says Pal.

"I know, Pal," I tell him. "But he's the only person at school who even talks to me. Everyone else —"

"I talk," he says.

I could tell him that he doesn't know what it's like to be a twelve-year-old girl, to feel so much older than everyone in your class and want so badly to be just like them. I could tell him I just want to be normal. That Evander is the closest to normal that I could find. But I don't know what it's like to have been Pal and then to lose everything. I don't know what it's like to be a full-grown man and have to rely on a little girl to wipe his butt. "You're a good talker, Pal," I assure him.

"No," I told her. "It's just us."

I must have sounded like that was the worst thing in the world, for it to be just us, because she said, "We'll we're going to find you a safe place to stay, Selena."

There were no sounds from inside the house except that giant clock that always buzzed in the kitchen. A bird landed on the shed behind the lady. A blue jay. "Shoot him," Pal would say when the jay would land close to the house. He was a pretty bird, but he always scared off the little finches. A car pulled out of our driveway. A jet way up in the sky flying somewhere better than here. Dried grass under the lady's shoes. My stomach.

"You need a bath," I say.

"Bubbles," says Pal.

"No bubbles," I tell him. "They give you a rash. And no tomato soup."

"Poop soup," says Pal.

"You're hilarious."

I fill up the tub just halfway with warm water. I'll wait until I've got him into the tub to add the hot water and make it cozy for him. I add just a few drops of shampoo to make a bubble bath.

The lady led me around the house to the driveway where her car was parked. The man was standing by the car talking on his phone.

"Where's Pal?" I asked.

"Mr. Jeffreys? The police – " the man began, but the lady interrupted him.

"They're taking him someone safe so he can get the care he needs."

"Like a hospital?" I asked.

"Yes," she said.

"There's foods he can't eat, and he gets rashes, and sometimes he chokes, and he –"

The lady kneeled down in front of me and took both my hands. "We're going to make sure Pal gets the best care," she said. "The best."

"You like Orange Julius?" asked the man.

Pal comes with me to the store to get diapers. He has run out, and it's never good when we run out. We are rolling down Spring Street. The sidewalks are brand new and really straight, so I sit in Pal's lap with the diapers in mine and let him work the chair. He works it at home fine, but if he's going fast or at the store, it's better if I do it so he doesn't run into things. Anyway, Spring Street is almost all flat, so I know we weren't going to be rocket fast. We are beboppin down the sidewalks – that's something Pal used to say – and Pal is keeping the chair straight. Only we are getting really close to the curve where the street branches. I tell Pal to slow down, but he just keeps going. He is laughing, so I start laughing. I am laughing but I am also scared because I don't want to have to get Pal back into his chair in someone's front yard, and I really don't want to end up in the street.

Pal puts his arms up in the air like he is flying, only his arms don't really straighten out. I tell him all the time he looks like an orangutan. He just makes woo hoo hoo noises.

Then he yells something that sounds like "flying orangutan," and he woo hoo hoos. And just before we are about to either crash into the street or have to somehow turn onto Spring Court, Pal grabs the wheels of the chair and stops us.

For a second, we are both quiet. I am holding onto Pal's pants legs. The box of diapers has tumbled into the grass. I look back at him, and his eyes are ginormous. Then we just both crack up together. There we are on the street corner, just down from the Kroger, hootin and hollerin as all the cars in the world drive past. "That's the stuff," Pal would have said. Maybe he tries to, only it sounds like, "Tough."

"Yeah," I told him. "We're tough."

"No fear," he calls.

"You said it, Pal," I say.

Then he pees all over everything.

Will Neal

Will Neal is a South London-born writer and investigative journalist based in Sarajevo. He has written for the Organised Crime and Corruption Reporting Project, *The Guardian,* VICE UK, *The Sunday Times* and *Novara Media.* His short fiction has been published with the Anglo-American literary magazine, *Litro.*

Interdependence

They leave the city in a borrowed van. It is an old model. Early nineties, three-seat cabin. The matt black of the exterior is faded and the rear side door is rusting and inside the seats are worn and the handle of the gearstick has come loose. Bits of rubber from the cracked dashboard have been collected into the cup holder above the hole where the radio was. There are strays scattered in the footwells. Cans of wiper fluid and oil sit in the pocket on the passenger side. Stickers form a patchwork across the bonnet and the rear-view mirror is held in place with tape. The air-freshener scentless and bleached near-white. Packing in hurried excitement they have not brought much. On the striped mattress stuffed into the back are their bags and a blanket and sheet. Two bottles of wine and one of gin. The plywood is cheap and new. Measurements sketched in pencil. The faint odour of sawdust.

They turn off the circular and follow the ramp up to the overpass. In the early morning the lights of the cranes and the towers shine and blink behind them. The high-rises ahead islanded by the low sprawl of houses. In the settlement below the portacabins stand neatly arranged. Boxed-in by shipping containers and cannibalised cars and concrete pillars. Plastic bags rustle like broken static on the fences and television antennas. Children weave on bikes between puddles hiding potholes, chasing the dogs chasing pigeons. Frisbees and half-deflated footballs gathering moss on the corrugated rain-shelters beside the wall that separates the camp and the legs of the pylons. When it gets dark there will be fires and noise late into the night. Until the squatters turn in, or the police are called.

The van shudders up a gear and hums as they pull onto the motorway. The lanes are almost empty. Joel shouts and thumps the dashboard and Alice's yawn breaks into laughter. She dabs her eye with the cuff of her fleece and leans over placing her hand at the back of his head, scratching gently. They enter and emerge from a tunnel under steady waves of orange light. He nods toward her feet and she removes her seatbelt to reach across and passes him a coffee in a ribbed dark red paper cup. She finishes her own and picking at it tears the outer layer off and into a strip which she gives a half-twist, fastening the ends with the gum residue and deciding she likes the little one-sided loop. Tacking it to the fan with a hairpin. She shuffles into the seat by the window. Curling up under her coat and fixing her gaze on a point ahead, below the corner of the wing mirror. The legs of the barrier flicker and disappear as the car picks up speed. A band of metal trembling in the air.

The sun breaks through. Alice dozes. When she wakes to stretch and sit up it is mid-afternoon. Joel taps a half-rhythm on the wheel. She asks where they are and he says he isn't sure. They left the motorway about an hour ago and are now in open country. There are no signs or telephone wires. Grass lines the road and then a steep ditch on either side separating them from fields of yellow flowers that stretch for miles around.

He opens his window. The air in the cabin begins to thrum. She opens hers too. She asks if he is hungry. He says he could eat. There has been nothing for the last few miles but they will keep an eye out at the next town. From where she is sitting the sun catches in his hair like threads of dark gold. He squints as he concentrates on the road because they have not stopped since they left the city and his glasses are in his bag in the back. He blinks in the light and at the road ahead. He has not shaved and around the slim lines of his mouth a few sharp dark hairs show through. An agitated warmth glows in her chest and she smiles and tells him she is happy to take over if he can find somewhere to stop.

In among the flowers some hundred meters back from the road at the end of a dirt track she stands over him and pulls up the hem of her thin dress. Hair dark against the cream of her thighs, the fact of her wanting making her want him that much more. Desire growing with desire. Gently pinning him down she remains there for a few moments afterwards, breathing and laughing softly. When she rolls off they lie side by side on the blanket, both naked from the waist down. He places his hand under his head, catching his finger and turning to see the inside of the wheel traced by a line of dark red ants. He watches the insects move. Fixed on their course and carrying bits of detritus their scurrying comes together to form a single, slowly stirring shape. Alice says it is funny, little links in a chain all playing their part such that they become something bigger and with a purpose greater than any one of them or maybe even all of them because what they do together is different even from when you take all at the same time what each of them does on their own. Like neurons in a brain. Joel doesn't follow. He agrees it is a nice idea. In the dying light and the warm evening air the crickets chirrup and rattle and sing.

At the sound of the engine and the tires on the tarmac small birds scatter carving erratic arcs above the fields and ribbons of colour flashing in the spray of the sprinklers. Heading in the opposite direction a car passes and then a sign that is new that tells them that in two miles they will turn left to cut through the trees which appear ahead as they reach the crest of a small hill. The road becomes looser and the gravel crackles and spits at the underside of the van.

In the shade it is cool. Joel rolls up his window and asks Alice to do hers. Pulling his phone from his jacket he checks the time and is surprised at how late it is and says that soon they will need to start looking for a place to eat.

The town makes a change. They pull into the car park and as Joel retrieves a few things from the back he notices that it is almost empty. In fact since the car a few miles back there has been no one else. No walkers in the forest. No-one wandering between shops. Though there are a few houses that fit the scenery and a tall church at the end of the main drag there are signs of wear. Long grass by the playground. Flyers from a few years before.

The lighting inside the hotel is cheap and thin. There is a large fireplace and wooden beams cross the low ceiling and it has some charm even if it is also deserted. Joel is thinking there must be a hundred other places like it and that there may be somewhere better just down the street when Alice rings the bell and a short man with greying hair and an earnest smile appears in a rush of noise and fuss. He tells them to sit wherever and he'll be over to take their drinks shortly before walking them to a table by the window and asking what he can get them. They ask for gin and he is back just as soon as he is gone, making a show of placing serviettes between the paper tablecloths and the base of the glasses though they quickly soak through in a wet ring. Alice raises her eyebrows and they touch glasses and try not to laugh when she points out that he is now waiting at reception and pretending not to watch them for any sign they are ready. When they are he is friendly and tells them he would have chosen the same. He returns sometime later. Sweating and with a dirty rag thrown over his shoulder. Joel jokes he is working the kitchen himself and Alice says it wouldn't surprise her if he was the only person here. He sits with them after they have eaten and offers them whisky or whatever they prefer, on the house. Joel says it is kind and he really doesn't have to go to any trouble and when Alice says that actually she'd like a brandy he pauses and says he would like one too. The manager tells them he is usually not left to himself like this and Alice asks why and Joel soon stops listening. Tuning in again when Alice says they'll take a room for the evening, nodding and saying he doesn't mind, sure, if she'd like. When the manager leaves to fetch their keys she is apologetic and admits it is not what they'd planned but maybe just for the first night, having pushed to put the miles between them and the city. He says again sure, if that's what she'd like.

When they turn in Alice feels sad. Joel thinks of how he would've been fine pitching up in the van.

They leave after a late breakfast. The yawning manager is relieved when they turn down a fry-up for coffee and toast. She settles up and does not mention to him or to Joel that the after-dinner drinks have found their way onto the tab. When Joel pulls up out front she says thanks and goodbye. Joel returns the manager's wave with a slight nod and as they pull away asks how weird was that guy and she says that actually she thought he was sweet. He says they probably need to put something in the tank and will she keep an eye out once they're back on the main road. She suggests they could take a look at the map then too, if he'd like.

On the far side of the pumps is a garage and a fast-food place thick with the smell of onions and packed with truckers from the HGV park on the other side of the bridge that crosses over the carriageway. She leaves him with the van and goes off to find the toilets which are no more than a brick outhouse. The doors to both cubicles are missing and so she takes a few single tissues from the dispenser and sneaks into the bushes to squat among the cider cans and rubbers. There are clothes too, mouldy with rain. Somehow there are always clothes by the side of the road and at service stations. Places like this are not really places at all, she thinks, more the spaces between places. Cracks in the pavement, filling the gaps simply because gaps are there to be filled. Little wonder that things should get lost.

She heads inside to wash her hands. As she ties up her hair she sees her image reflected again in the dull mirror on the other side of the room and a row of her arms moving simultaneously one behind the other. Endless Alice, caught in a corridor of frames making the small space seem much larger than it is. She feels dizzy. Like looking down from too far up.

Joel sits in the cabin and sees her walking over. She catches his eye and smiles and he smiles back and as she gets closer he can see the dark mole that marks where the line of her jaw meets her chin. She climbs into the cabin and he notices that she's wearing his threadbare woollen jumper. The dark green one she's always liked.

It strikes him that perhaps he might be happy with this woman for a long time. That this might be the moment he later tells people about, the moment on that trip they took on the morning after that party, when he saw her come out of the services wearing his jumper with the mole where her jaw meets her chin. When she got into the car smiling with the tattoo on the nape of her neck visible between the collar at the back and the stray hairs of a loose bun. When she kissed him on the cheek and belted herself in and asked why they weren't already gone.

He folds the map and says if they keep heading west they'll eventually hit the coast. Sounds like a plan, she says. We could even stop for a swim.

They drive in silence. She asks if everything is alright and he says he is a little tired. When she offers to swap over he tells her not to worry, that they'll be there before too long. She talks about the sea and a family holiday when she was young. He nods along and she soon goes quiet, settling into her spot by the passenger window.

Outside the light begins to change. Subtle, but certain. Around them the banks of the carriageway slope upward in sharp focus, the grass shining vivid and waving with the passing of the cars. Through the heat the rays of the sun take on a razored edge and at the distorted ends of their reach the sky appears as if from behind a film of soap, rich with the shades between green and purple. The clouds orange and pink like ink sinking thinly through water and among them a sense of growing movement somewhere deep in the atmosphere, the air charged with the early electricity of a gathering storm despite the brightness of the afternoon. An hour passes and Joel parks in a layby at the foot of the path leading to the clifftop and as Alice gets changed in the back he clambers onto the roof and sits looking out at the waves and the strange brilliance above. She makes to join him and he slips forward down the windscreen and sets off along the path asking if she is ready. Locking the doors she jogs to catch him almost halfway up the hill.

They reach the top. Alice admits to herself it is not unusual for Joel to behave like this and walks on ahead. She swings her arms and breathes deeply and takes in the cool and the salt and the smell of rot and froth and goes off the idea of swimming and thinks instead she would like to keep walking. The ground is soft and dry. She would go barefoot were it not for the thorns and the gorse where the path narrows here and there. Levelling out it runs flat for another few miles and after an hour or two leads them inland and then slopes down toward a beach where there are small wooden huts and picnic blankets and horse tracks along the shoreline, children playing in the shallows. A flight of stone steps marks the start of the promenade. There are restaurants and stalls and an arcade and kiosks selling tickets to the fairground along the pier that juts out awkwardly beyond the lip of the cliff at the far end of the cove.

The way down is steep and winding. By the time they step out onto the beach the sun has arced and casts a vicious and injured red across the bay and boats. Trembling as it kisses and is swallowed by the sea. The families have packed away, replaced by groups gathering around glowing fires and music from speakers. Hammocks bowed between vans driven out onto the shore. A few teenagers in bright yellow polo shirts and blue shorts bring in the last of the sunloungers and stash them in a stumpy building behind the wooden fence. They are paid by a bald man who sits smoking in the blue light of a portable television under an umbrella fixed in concrete under the sand.

Alice and Joel climb the steps. The restaurant fronts are well-lit against the blue-black of the late evening. Somewhere a band plays. Garlic and salt and spices hang deliciously in the air. At the stalls there are fish nestled in piles of wet ice between lemons and shells. Their eyes clouded grey with grillsmoke. It is busy. Customers sit sweating at white plastic tables drinking and eating off of checked tablecloths, cats darting across the wooden floor and between their legs. Picking at scraps. There's a wordless decision neither much want a spot by the fair or the arcade. They take a table at a bar toward the middle of the boardwalk. The place is small and a woman with red hair brings them their drinks and some olives and otherwise leaves them alone.

Over empty bottles and defleshed stones Alice asks Joel to talk to her.

He asks what she would like to talk about. She says he can do her the decency of not pretending like nothing is wrong. That he's tired isn't going to cut it because together they made the decision to go and she's been travelling just the same. Wherever the band started out they are getting closer. She is surprised that he really doesn't know what she's talking about, that not every moment has to be filled. It pisses her off and she tells him so, that no, not every moment needs to be filled with talk but that he is fine filling every moment when they're around other people might suggest that they could maybe have filled a few today. Joel says he just thinks it kind of sad when people feel the need to say something and can't be happy just being together. She sits back and is hurt. The music is getting louder and there are horns too and Alice tells Joel that it's a really gross take on what she was saying. The melody and cymbals are growing and when the accordionist looms into view with all the calm of the walk now gone and the hurt in its place she tells him that fuck this for a laugh she'll give him all the peace and quiet he can handle. They finish the second song and he drops a few coins into the flatcap and the accordionist says thanks and he realises she isn't coming back. He motions at the redhaired woman who clears the table and when he does not follow after Alice she brings another bottle and places it in front of him. Her hand on his shoulder as she returns to the dim interior.

Joel sits for a long time. When he leaves the stalls are closing. The ground is uneven beneath his feet. The boardwalk stretches further than he remembers and on the beach the fires have grown tall. Shadows play across the sand and standing at the top of the steps he listens to the low voices and the music made distant by the wash of the water. He considers joining them and knows that if anything will make this impossible to fix it is that. He feels alone, and at the thought of Alice lying awake and furious in the van comes a sudden flood of regret. She is right. He has been resentful and sullen and like a child and infantile was the word she had used and for what? Of course she is right and the embarrassment at being wrong and unable to remember why it is he has been bitter only adds to his remorse, the regret growing with the shame of it and of not remembering and at having cause to be ashamed at all. Hoping that perhaps she is not already asleep he pays the bald man under the umbrella for another two bottles from the blue and white cool-box and sets off unsteadily toward the path. It is gone two. It occurs to him she may even have been upset enough to have left altogether.

A hard wind blows through the gorse and Joel is not cold. He is drunk. His feet fall heavy and in an uncertain rhythm and his eyelids are heavy too. There is a pounding in his head and the wind is singing and it is loud and there is the smell of rot and froth from the waves below. In the bay the boats dip and roll and farther out the sea is calm and empty and so very empty and his head is pounding. He rolls his ankle and stumbles but does not fall and goes along hopping and cursing. He tests his weight and it aches and sends a pain through his leg and into his gut and on the ground he falls and rests with his hand against his temple and the pressure around his eye and the pounding in his head and the ground beginning to tilt as he lies back feeling like he is holding on for dear life to nothing much at all. There is acid in his heart and the taste of bile. Above him the saturated shapes have gone and now the stars arrayed in cold intensity, their bright refractions enough to split but somehow not brighten the ink-black blanket as though the brightness of each had reached out a celestial finger and joined with the next and the next and the next along the shortest line of departure so that the night resembles not a map of constellations but a geometric chart of shining points across that domed surface and still, still the darkness between and impenetrable. An absolute nothing against a phantom and irregular spider's web making a curved surface of infinite distance, nothing beyond the stars and the black and the roads of light between them. It is beautiful and strange and unlike anything he has ever seen and Joel thinks that it is beautiful and like nothing he has seen. Between the pounding in his head and tilting of the ground with the wind singing loud and the smell of rot and froth he is held fast, stuck between the nothing of the sky and the odour of the air and the motion of the earth. He is held in place, fixed by that unknown and alien beauty far above and beyond and yet so near until with a sudden convulsion and noise that especially to him sounds pitiable and mournful he leans and vomits quietly over the grass beside him. Lying on the mattress in the van he whispers that he is sorry. He is quite drunk.

The thud comes like a fall to earth. Rising sleep-blind in the dark he panics and recognises the pothole on the track from the day before and realises she is not beside him but already up as she is now driving them on. There is little he can do beyond tapping on the board by his head and waiting for what he assumes is her finding a place to stop. He lies rocking and jolting with the van and feels his tongue dry and fetid and his eyes hot and stinging. He hopes she was not awake when he got back. It is a slim chance but one he will take that she slept through and that he may be able to play sharp and sleep off the fog before they get anywhere by early to late afternoon.

Alice takes her time stopping. He knows she has heard him and is taking her time with great purpose because there were any number of sideroads and widenings they passed on the way from the motorway the day before and he knocked well before the crackling and bumping under him became smooth and besides she might have stopped in the middle of the track and let him out. He lies in the motion of the darkness and waits with the swelling nausea and the growing smell of himself unwashed and by the time she finds somewhere he has lost hope of keeping it from her but when she flings open the doors and stands before him she seems in good spirits and when she kisses him he thinks that she must know it and sees that it does not appear to bother her much at all. She offers him a baked flapjack and an iced tea they bought at the services and tells him to follow when he is ready. Climbing on top of the cabin. He listens to her hands and knees on the thin buckling metal of the roof.

They sit side by side by the side of a road winding at a great height. Where there had been ocean and sand there is now a drop and tall sharp hills dense with ferns broken by copses and outcrops. A range of snowy caps far beyond. Perhaps the thud was not the pothole and perhaps they have come many miles since and still he cannot understand so dramatic a change in such a short time as though they have entered another part of the country entirely. It is humid and not yet raining though the air is thick with it. He eats gingerly and says that he is sorry that they fought. She seems to shrug and tells him there is a sign for a waterfall and that she'd like to walk. She is wearing her waterproof and boots. Inwardly he is grateful because his head is like glass and crashing he has started to shiver though the sugar of the tea has helped some.

They climb the path part-step part-slope and before long reach the water falling against the rocks a short distance away. Following the stream they arrive at a wide pool. As he sits and catches his breath with his head swimming she strips down and steps into the water which is warm. Moving slow and measured like a pale creature of lithe beauty bathing and watchful she swims to the far side and back and calls him in and reaches him as he finishes undressing to take him by the hand and guide him through the shallows and up above his waist where he gasps at the water not quite warm enough. She presses her mouth to his and wraps her arms around his neck and one leg about him and then the other so that she is astride him standing in the centre of the pool. The air hangs heavy and thick with the not-yet rain and if the first time after they had left in the field surrounded by flowers it was tender here among the trees and the rocks and embraced by the water it is filled with quiet anger and force, a rush of aggression running deep through her and rapidly deepening and fuelled by his passiveness such that she can with only a slight gesture or shifting of her weight drive his movements as though he is following her own, as though through some power his body has become a part of her own the dark engine in his skull firing with hers the mirrored image of bursts of sparks and shots and as she presses her fingers white against his dark skin and his head between her breasts and as she tightens about him and calls out and her cry is lost to the trees there is a movement in the water and in the ground as stones work loose from the hanging rock to fall and it is shaking as the earth moves out and away from under them and throwing back and forth now with a terrible violence and they two encircled in the shivering water in the midst of it clasped together with her eyes closed against the tumult as if waiting for the world to break and twist and tear around them enveloping a new and destructive heart. She breathes and all is still. Joel feels as though he might pass out.

He lies in the water as she returns to the bank and gets dressed and when he wades over and begins to pick through his clothes she starts wordlessly through the trees leaving him hopping into his shorts and sandals and calling after her.

They drive through the night. Coming down to the wide valley and then the plain that stretches on toward the foot of the mountains. The two-lane road is narrow and cuts straight like a knife through the barren landscape which is dust and rock and darkness. The stars are out again. As they leave the hills and the water and the grass behind them something gives in the engine and becomes at first a whine and then a howl. They stop and pop the hood and change over and drive on making a note to stop somewhere as soon as they can though there is nowhere ahead and behind them only the night and in the tail-lights the red dust rising. The dashboard shudders with the pained noise of the engine and with it the strip fastened by gum and Alice's hairpin, the road rising up to meet them like a conveyor belt through the monotony of that flattened and desolate place and changing over every few hours from passenger side to driver and back the mountains growing larger and yet still so much further a way to go. The grinding of the wheels and the stars in their cold and web-like array and the howling engine and the cans and bottles agitated in the pockets of the doors and the roaring through the vents in the dashboard growing harsher and louder until the sky as if hit by a giant and invisible object with a great and unimaginable force in a sudden explosion and silent is seen to split along its ghostly fault-lines, the surface of the world above shattered like a glass pane and shards in free-fall floating like the geometric fragments of a kaleidoscope far above the wheeled and speeding black box running not through time or space but across their rolling surface the scenery repeating the same rock the same fence and ruined building the bleached remainder of some engine some tanker some animal some frame some unknown form abandoned to the mercilessness of the sun in the day of that place and its deathly lords at night and over and again to the marking rumble of high speed and shrieking of the engine and the gearstick jerking and they are set along a strange course along a strange loop with the mountains before them like starved dogs after a scrap of meat on a length of string at the end of a stick and fixed ahead with the scenery self-same passing all around them between the here and the there that is the faraway nearby between the edges of chaos penned back by the thin metal band that trembles by the van and remains constant and uninterrupted and unending so that there is only motion only the change of the same after the same and the sky in shards falling and the back and forth of changing over without memory of stopping only an unceasing oscillating inverting along the path of constant change from same to same along the knife of the trail along which they are following after the before and leading before the after as the ants around the hubcap as the firing in their skulls as the arms of endless Alice in the mirror and the shame and desire and the earth in revolt and semen in the water and the colours bleeding across the rays of the sun and the clouds. There is hurt and sex and anger and remorse and loving and they two together in the cabin as the world heaves and speeds and falls around them. The sky is falling. The sky is falling and there is nothing in that night but the speeding through it they two together in the cabin and the changing sameness and the falling of the sky.

Alice sits waiting at the station. They had driven through the night because Joel insisted they get the engine sorted. As dawn broke over the peaks they arrived at a small town where the mountains began. Joel pulled in at the garage and talked with the mechanic who looked and hopped into the cabin to listen. He told them that the whining was likely the need of new fluid. The transmission might need replacing. This would take time. It was also expensive.

Left alone as Joel followed him inside she realised it was turning into a bad trip. It'd seemed such an adventure when they'd first had the idea. Playing with the torn coating of the old coffee cup she clipped back her hair with the pin and thought of how it came to them. Spontaneously at a house party two nights before they left. Being between jobs to take off and go for as long as the money held out. Joel had called his brother who had said it was ok now he'd bought the hatchback but to drive easy because it wasn't what it once was. And just like that they were gone.

Through the window of the building she saw Joel beginning to argue. From the way he moved his hands she could tell it was not going well. His palm against his forehead, his brows raised and eyes closed and the dark circles from lack of sleep. His shorts patched green by the moss of the rocks by the pool. Perhaps the grass on the cliffs above the beach. In her hand the gum of the card came loose and leaving the broken strip on the seat behind her she had climbed out of the cabin and taken her backpack and walked to the station where she bought a ticket and where she is now waiting at the platform. She is waiting and by the time he has looked and not found her and called and gone to voicemail the train will have left and will be carrying her back to the city. It will be carrying her home.

Makena Onjerika

Makena Onjerika won the 2018 Caine Prize for African Writing. Her work has appeared or is forthcoming in *Granta, Johannesburg Review of Books, Fireside Quarterly, Wasafiri, Waxwing, Jalada, New Daughters of Africa, Doek!, DRR* and others. She runs the Nairobi Fiction Writing Workshop and recently published the workshop's first anthology, *Digital Bedbugs*. She writes both realist literary fiction and speculative fiction.

Girl Games

A centrifugal force binds them. Gweng to Madam. Madam to Gweng. They dance on a Friday mid-morning, and sunlight licks the concrete courtyard at the center of the building with its large burning tongue and sets them aflame. Their shadows intertwine. Gweng's red skirt blooms, long black legs skipping underneath as Madam's leather belt raises its head and bites skin with a flat sound, paa, paa, paa. And from the dark hole of Gweng's mouth come screams, and words you do not understand. Maybe she is calling her mother; maybe she is calling God. Maybe she is cursing. You feel irritation at her for not taking this beating as she should: quietly. She did say terrible things.

They rip apart and Gweng flies, a stone off a slingshot aimed at the gate. And in that moment, she exits your life. Later, you will search your memories for her, you will squint into the past, you will scour through it as one does rice for pebbles, but you will not find even a blurred image or an echo of her.

She escapes and you remain behind in the shadow and under the weight of five floors of rental housing. Above, on the verandas facing the courtyard, househelps and stay-at-home mums who left their washing, cooking and minding of babies to witness Gweng's beating are now whispering. It is from their angry eyes that you realize you have done something wrong. You begin to tremble where you squat watching Madam wash her hands. You do not resist when your househelp Scola grabs you by the arm and forces you indoors.

There, behind glass panes separating you from the good children, from life itself, you are kept company by your dread. You know exactly what will happen when Maami returns from her office job in the evening. She will take off her shoes; she will wash her face; she will pull out her brassiere from under her blouse through an armhole; she will settle down to her evening meal; she will ask Scola for a glass of water and switch on the red Greatwall TV for the nine o'clock news. Then, Scola will ensure you receive the beating of your life.

A story is told:

The mothers said to their children, do not go to the forest in the sky. The fathers said to the children, go anywhere but the forest in the sky. The grandmothers and grandfathers too. But the children giggled because surely, there was no forest in the sky.

Then, one day, the children went to fetch water at the river, something they did every day. They knew the path very well, but you know how the world changes. Trees pull up their roots and walk; mountains fall into valleys; rivers go visiting their friends in faraway lands. The children got lost.

One of them said, let us wait here; the elders will surely come and find us, but the others were eager to explore this new, strange land. They left the familiar riverbank and went to see where all the mist covering the ground came from. As though the clouds had fallen from the sky, they said one to another.

The ogre found them eating from his orchard and let them engorge themselves until their tummies swelled with mango. When they were languid, he roared and jumped from his hiding place. He pursued them everywhere in that forest, his footsteps thundering across the sky, his eyes flashing lightning as he sought them among the clouds, and the children's tears rained down on earth.

He is still seeking and eating them one by one. And they are still crying.

Gweng and her people enter your consciousness, one day, like figures emerging from the distorting white heat of desert. You do not understand how they could have been present in your life all along, carrying such stark difference, yet unnoticed by you. You form them in your mind as the sum total of very black and very tall. Noticing them is akin to discovering the proper pronunciation of a familiar word.

When you ask Scola about them, she spits two words at you: 'Sudanese' and 'refugees'. Words you move about in your mouth, testing with your teeth, rolling on your tongue.

The strong smell of fish emanating from Gweng's house next door leaves Scola both nauseous and cantankerous. She bangs pots and shouts and pulls your ears for real and imagined transgressions. Your own fish, filleted and fried in onion and tomato, smells nothing like fish.

There are many foods Scola finds revolting – jam which she says looks like old blood and the sticky mrenda people in Western Kenya eat – snail vegetable, she calls it. You understand Scola is like this because she grew up in ushago, in Meru, where she ate only maize, beans and potatoes every day. Her tongue refuses to venture beyond its white fence; her stomach rejects the unknown. You pity her: she will never know the cold painful sweetness of ice cream, the sour tingle of maziwa mala or the salty cottoniness of popcorn. You know you must hide your six-year-old delight from her insular judgment, be it the white, chalky joy of Patco sweets you sneak into bed and crunch into your teeth under your blanket or be it Gweng.

Long-necked Gweng. Her neck lifts her round face like a sunflower. You imagine rubbing her black skin to a shine with paraffin and crumpled newspaper the way Maami has Scola clean the glass panes on the windows. You want Gweng's laughter, that crackling outburst, a large bird calling from its perch on a telephone cable above your street. You want her red dress and her orange dress because they make her seem aflame. You want her name with its sharp curtailed sound at the end, so much better than the one you inherited from your grandmother.

Watch her dodge the ball in a game of Kaati. Standing between the two ball throwers, her legs are slightly bent at the knees and her skirts lifted. She is a wound-up spring. Her eyes shine. Then the throws begin, and the two ball throwers try in vain to hit her with the ball. It moves in a blur and her body swims around it, curving backwards and out so that the ball rips just past her belly. She flies; she slides; she twists; she is boneless. The throwers fling faster and harder. Gweng throws herself against the dusty ground. Your insides jump up to your throat; you could explode from the tension of these moments. Gweng's team is in a frenzy. Their bodies mimic hers around imaginary balls. She wins after fifty throws. Everyone goes mad. You scream yourself raw.

Your older brother Kim has always included you in his boy games. You have mastered the Mfaraa: how to set the thin wire wheel moving; how to flick the stick attached to it by string to keep it upright and spinning; how to bend it to your will so that it takes sharp turns. You know tree climbing and you know Banoo: you hold your mottled marble at the tip of your index finger, draw the finger back and release to knock your opponents' marbles tidily into the Banoo hole.

But Kim cannot teach you how to play girl games: not skip rope or Bladaa, not ChaMama or hopscotch. You receive no cheers in Kaati. The other girls do not want you in their teams.

You orbit Gweng and her Sudanese friends as they move across the street, from their universe into yours and back, joining games as they please then withdrawing into a tight cluster of whispered secrets against one of the walls of the buildings in your street. You want their strange, fast language. You want to cut off others with foreign words as they do, and laugh large, all white teeth on display. But they will not admit you or even notice your longing.

One afternoon, the tailorwoman at Ebenezer Tailoring sets her Singer machine spinning and whistling. Then she leans towards the customers sitting on a bench in her shop waiting for their clothes. She has heard from someone who heard from someone else that the Sudanese escaped their country with bagfuls of gold.

'They don't live like people who have suffered,' chimes in the electronics repairman from next door.

You know that refugees live in tents made of polythene bags and sticks and have the look of being startled out of sleep. You have seen them on CNN. Dust blurs their emaciated faces, and they are always staring into the distance helplessly as their bodies wilt into skin and bone. They escape war on godforsaken roads with the remnants of their lives balancing on their heads: pots, rolled-up mattresses, bits of clothing. Their children have flies licking sores at the corners of their mouths. Their eyes are large in their dry, leathery faces. Time decays as they walk. When they arrive in Nairobi, Gweng is four years behind in school and in the same standard one class as you. Thinking of all Gweng must have endured brings tears to your eyes in the middle of the night, and you cry quietly into Scola's back in your shared bed. You wish you had suffered as much and bite down on your tongue to feel some of Gweng's pain.

You sneak up to the open kitchen window of her house one afternoon, hide under its jutting sill and listen until you are certain there is no one within. You rise to your toes and take a peek. You don't expect to see gold – Gweng and her family live six in this two-bedroom house – but what you do see is disappointing and not very different from your own: stainless steel sufurias, a cooking stick jutting out of a basin piled high with dirty dishes, a dying charcoal stove. The room is a cave of soot. A low stool stands guard in the corner, two dips worn into its wooden top to accommodate buttocks. This is where Gweng's mother sits, orchestrating her meals.

'What are you doing?'

You jump. A light brown face is staring down at you from between two vertical rods in the stairs' bannister. You become conscious of your wrinkled clothes. You already have two patches of dirt on your trousers' knees. She is wearing lace-fringed socks and red pumps and a dress Maami would never let you take outside unless it was a Sunday and you were headed to church.

'You were spying,' she says and beats her index finger on her middle finger in the universal gesture for you-are-in-trouble.

You fold your arms across your chest. You don't like this one but feel the need to explain. 'I was looking for my friend.'

The girl frowns. 'That long Sudanese is your friend?'

'Yes,' you hear yourself say even as your little heart clenches. Then you flee, and your rubber Bata slippers go tapa tapa tapa on the concrete all the way to the gate.

Gweng notices you only once. You are furiously digging a hole on the other side of the street from her, determined to play some game of your own making because Kim and his friends will not play with you today. Gweng beckons and you drop your stick and wipe your muddy hands on your skirt. Your throat is dry as you bring your ear close to her mouth.

'You are showing everyone your red panties. The boys are laughing at you,' she says.

Your heart falls stone-heavy into your belly. The only way to save face is to linger and pretend to the world you are not soaking in shame, dripping with the mud of it.

Besides, a new want has wiggled into your body. Gweng and her friends each have a handmade doll, soft bodies of leftover kitenge print cloth, with stitched-on black faces, buttons for eyes and thick woollen string for hair. Your want is an intense bittersweet taste in your mouth, the bite and sugar of tamarind. Your want is a tightening knot in your belly.

Gweng frowns when you ask. 'You can't buy these,' she says. 'Our Auntie made them.'

Maami has promised you one of the dolls on the shelves of Safeway supermarket, but your birthday is months, no, centuries away. And so you steal bits of cloth from among Maami's things. You tuck them into your panties and smuggle them out of the house and out the gate. You are breathless as you pull down your underwear. But Gweng will not touch your bits of hope. They have been in dirty, stinking places.

You and Kim are prone to transgression and misbehaviour, and this is why Maami has a leather belt hanging on a hook behind her bedroom door. It was you who broke her red love-heart clock after she said never to play with it. You who tried to iron a brand-new Sunday-best and burnt a hole in its hem. You who wets the bed you share with Scola, night after night. You who commented about Kim's yellow shoes being girly and made him refuse to wear them ever again, even though Maami spent three-thousand shillings on them. There is a badness in you. Long before you betray Gweng, you crush a chick with a pole and hear its bones crunch. Then you prod it with a toe and squat and prod it with a finger. It refuses to get up. A strange, unsettling feeling seizes you. You run to Scola and nag her into following you back to the chick.

'This girl, don't you know what you have done?'

She is not annoyed. Her eyes are full of pity. You understand she cannot save you from what you've done.

'You have removed its life,' she says.

You look around for the chick's life.

'No. You cannot make it come alive again.'

You shake your head. You step back. Urine snakes down your leg and pools in your shoe.

Another story is told. You have heard this one, no? It's a running joke in the newspapers:

Once upon a time, when God was an old man, he decided he was quite tired of his wife. She had the unfortunate problem of a sharp tongue. With it, she had reduced him to a patch of shade outside his own hut. And so, in retaliation, he dug up some clay and made humans so that they would love him and sing his praises day and night. But as soon as he put them in his kiln to bake, his wife's stew of the previous night began boiling in his stomach, and he dashed into the latrine. By the time he emerged again, his first humans were burnt to a crisp black. He clucked his tongue and threw them over his shoulder, and ever since, they have had only his back to look upon.

The light-brown girl from upstairs is Ivy. You become friends because she is too clean to play Kaati or Bladaa or skip-rope. When you are knocked out of a game of Kaati after two throws, she is standing at the gate, eyes darting this way and that after the children in the street.

'I have many dolls,' she says.

You think she is bragging, but quickly recognize that this is an invitation and an apology for upsetting you the other day.

'How many?'

Five. And they eclipse anything you have ever wanted. Ivy pulls her dollhouse into the fifth-floor veranda to let you play (because her mother has said to never, ever allow anyone into their house).

Her dolls are blond and white and slender. They have joints at the knees and elbows, not just at the hips and shoulders. They blink. They sit on the dollhouse's miniature chairs, and if you pull a string in their backs, they speak. Each comes with five dresses and combs that go into neat little drawers. You work hard at not looking surprised or jealous.

'My daddy bought it for me,' says Ivy.

Perhaps she knows about your family; perhaps she does not. Her pride cuts you with something hot. She has touched a spot you protect with kicks and bites. You could lunge at her and scratch off her face. Your voice drops to a growl.

'You don't have a father.'

She giggles and recklessly pushes you at the shoulder. 'Everyone has a father, silly. Even if he lives somewhere else.'

Her gesture, even more than her words, this show of easy playfulness, this repayment of kindness for your intended malice, this off-hand forgiveness, this is what makes you tell her things, many things.

What you hear Gweng say is nothing new. You too have heard some version of it before, from the househelps. But as you will come to understand much later, Ivy's mother cannot beat the househelps.

They do not notice you as they huddle at the communal water taps, their bodies like question marks over the washbasins. You are squatting under the stairs, watching them battle clothes into submission, drowning them in the frothy seas of wash water.

'The children have to call her Madam as if she were not their mother.'

'At ten p.m., drunk and shouting like madness.'

'Every week, a new man in the house.'

'Doesn't she care about the children?'

To Ivy, you add, 'And then Gweng said your mother is a malaya.'

This is meant to be your secret, something to bind you to each other. With it, you will exclude all others. But Ivy's face crumbles as if she were about to cry, and she goes into her house. Madam is smiling when she emerges a moment later. She pats you on the head.

'That Sudanese called me a prostitute?' she asks as she plucks something out of your hair as if you were dear to her, and she could not stand to have you untidy. 'Go bring her to me,' she says.

You let her whisper guide you down five flights of stairs, across the concrete courtyard and into the wild that is your street. Your brother Kim and his friends are throwing stones into a muddy pothole just to hear it gulp them, chubuliu! The twins from the third floor are tiptoeing towards Mzee, the goat who likes to graze on the street's garbage heaps, to try climb his back. And here are the unemployed men who sit on a bench outside KwaJoseph General Shop, buying cigarettes by the stick, throwing down cards with gusto in a game of Karata and whistling at any swinging behind that goes by. You swim through this melee and narrowly miss collision with a man flying down the street on a bicycle, his arms shaking from the effort of taming his two-wheeled beast and its load of bread crates. You skip over a perennial tickle of greenish muck, a union of wash water from the buildings on the street. Madam's voice compels you on.

You will be twenty years too late in realizing you should have done anything but lead Gweng to her judgement. You should have fled and hidden behind Scola. That giant of a woman would have protected you from all your mischief, albeit after pulling your ears hard. But no, you are full of badness, occupied by the devil himself.

'You know what people are calling you?' Scola asks when she imprisons you indoors to await Maami's punishment. 'A big, empty debe. Who taught you such bad manners?'

She looks at you the way Maami will this evening, as though she does not know you and you do not belong to her. You shout nonsense when Maami whips the gossiping devil out of you. Tomorrow other children in the building will laugh at the sounds you are making. Kim will illustrate your skipping, dodging and twisting to them. You will hide under the stairs again.

'I won't do it again,' you plead.

But Maami knows you still have much more pain to give and receive in this life. And she keeps whipping you to save you from yourself.

'You will return that girl's dolls, you hear? First thing tomorrow morning,' she says.

Up you go early the next day, climbing five flights of stairs. Madam comes to the door with a smile as broad as the leaves of a money tree, then wilts and shakes her head when you hold out Ivy's dolls.

'But you can have them as long as you like.' She calls into the house: 'Ivy, Kendi has come to play.'

This is what panic and grief look like. A woman gripping the frame of her door, shaking her head until it appears not to be a part of her body. You come to pity her. No other woman you knew back then wore trousers or stick-on nails painted red. She left the idlers at the general store spitting and cursing when her manual transmission Nissan pickup charged up the street with a plangent roar. Only she wore lipstick in the broad daylight. And had boyfriends in the space a husband had abandoned. A woman untamed. Every day she contended with a world that had no place for her. You see that now.

But you also remember that she had a basin of hot water brought down to her from the fifth floor after she beat Gweng. You remember her lips pulled back in a snarl as she made a show of washing her hands with bar soap, then washing powder, then disinfectant.

Susanne Stich

Originally from Nürnberg, Susanne Stich has lived in the Northwest of Ireland for many years. Her writing has appeared in *The Stinging Fly, Ambit, Bath Flash Fiction, TSS Publishing* and other magazines. In 2018 she was a finalist at the Irish Novel Fair and received a bursary award from the Irish Arts Council to work on her debut novel. She has worked in the arts and educational sector as a lecturer, curator and facilitator, and is currently Literary Guide at Verbal Arts Centre, Derry, where she curates literature for shared reading sessions in the community, promoting dialogue and wellbeing.

Unmappable

In November they appeared briefly in the beam of her headlights: blondes, redheads, brunettes, and various more daring dyes, bright blue or white. Plaits, bobs and boyish crops. Bare legs, skirts and blazers in sorry shades of brown, taupe, burgundy. Some stood alone, but most of them in groups. By February, with dawn arriving earlier, on dry, cloudless days there was a glow to them as early as ten past eight. The routine hasn't changed, even if it is March now. As soon as she spots them she slows down, enough to get a good look. A cop would do the same. Intuitive, some of the girls will notice that they're being watched. It will make them talk, spit, fantasize, but by the time they do their worst her car will have passed them.

Frauke. The Irish struggle with her name. Some make it sound like 'freak'. When she moved here sixteen years ago it made her giggle. She didn't know what was coming when she settled in the border region of Donegal and Derry, happy to pay with both Euro and Sterling.

'Like Frau K,' she told people, 'but don't say *kay*, make it a "k", short and sharp, like children learning to read, "k", "k", "k", like a sigh of disbelief, a single cough.'

During the sleepless nights her head buzzes with English language proverbs. *Fools rush in where angels fear to tread.* She obsesses over the perfect translation when often there isn't one. *Blinder Eifer schadet nur.* Don't be too keen, basically. It will harm you. In her case, it did.

The car is cold in the mornings. She keeps the radio off, preferring the sounds of the vehicle, the windscreen wipers on rainy days.

'What did you want when you were eleven?' the therapist asked last August.

It played in her head alongside the proverbs. *A bird in the hand is worth two in the bush.* She always wanted things. Everybody wants things. *Der Spatz in der Hand ist besser als die Taube auf dem Dach.* Compared with her thoughts, the driving is easy. Thirty years ago. God knows what she wanted back then. She's amazed how much make-up some of these girls wear, considering their age.

In the autumn, when the therapist suggested she step out a little, a peculiar time of year for such a thing, the first two weeks the clocks were still on summer time. The darkness did not swallow her, and when it did, that last weekend in October, Halloween looming, she told herself that the shock would wear off, vaccine-like. Down the line she'd be immune to something. Her hopefulness surprised her. Leave the house at 7:45, crawl up to the top of the estate, join the main road into town, drive on to Foyle Arena. The school year was in full swing. The girls must have been there all along, like the trees and lampposts along the way. It took the darkness for Frauke to notice them.

There are boys, too. They don't interest her. She's taught them in the classroom, knows their types. It is the girls who make her get up, cross the border, swim sixty laps. Afterwards she slides back into the other country, which, to her, leaving aside the locals' take on the matter, isn't another country really, but part of the big stew of Europe she grew up in, in another life.

In the beginning, border living, not unlike teaching, seemed like a dance, a charming sequence of steps while the past lay like insoles in everyone's shoes. Everyone had stories to tell. Different stories from the ones Frauke knew from home, yet not unlike them in the end. In these parts, telling a story means talking about the border. *The devil is in the details.* She's always had a philosophical streak, and not for a long time did Frauke think about what the border might do to her, this particular one, let alone the borders in her head, between full and depleted, young and middle-aged, peace and disquiet.

'This girl excels at history,' a teacher told her parents once.

When it came to choosing a career Frauke convinced herself that teaching was the one thing you could do anywhere. *A bird in the hand.*

'I'm running out of steam,' she told her husband last summer.

'You're taking this place to heart. You have to stop. There's a bigger world out there, and you know it. It's all about thinking long,' Dermot replied. They chuckled, as if it was just one of those things. Ireland, Northern Ireland, the universe. Afterwards, they watched a movie on Netflix, something they both agreed on, Spanish or French arthouse, a BBC drama perhaps, she can't remember now. The following morning he was back on the road, travelling across his native county, 'performing procedures', as he called it, on sheep, cows and horses, while Frauke returned to school across the border, where she taught German until nine months ago.

A few days later, the end of the school year looming, she sobbed in the toilet when she should have been in class, then walked out of the building, drove home. 'I won't go back,' she informed Dermot, and then, for a few days, she stopped talking altogether.

Schweigen ist Gold. Sometimes the proverbs translate well. *Silence is golden.* When it came to the word 'breakdown', the silence helped. She hated the term. It featured in her sick line, made Frauke think of a car.

There was no single reason for all this. She spent the long days of summer in pyjamas, scribbling into her journal, fragmented memories appearing like newsflashes. Airless school corridors, cracked mobile phone screens, boys being bullied in plain sight, false smiles in the staff room, colleagues bragging about fitness routines, boys obsessively drawing zombies and vampires, the TV at night, a smorgasbord of bunkum.

She had run out of patience long before, screamed in the classroom a few times. Her moods backfired, like the rubbish everywhere after break time. In the early years, when she caught boys dropping their litter, she confronted them about how long it would take for their plastic to dissolve. She smiled, almost flirted a little, anything to grab their attention.

'Forever! You and I will long be gone.'

There came a point when she stopped.

For god's sake.

Pupils watched as words formed in her mind, boys with crew cuts and acne, who kept asking 'why Hitler did what he did'.

'You're German. You must know,' she still hears them.

At mid-summer impossibility covered her life like thin ice. The waters below, a rage she didn't think possible, a toxic cocktail long imbibed, impossible to get out of her system. She took baths, poked at foam bubbles. When she finally spoke again, she could tell by the look in Dermot's eyes that he didn't understand a word she said.

'You don't think the same thing could have happened in Germany?'

he asked. Standing in her dressing gown, she shrugged, anger fluttering between flannel and skin. Oh, what had she done with her life?

In the background, the border hovered like a tightrope, all the years in Ireland too similar to tell apart, years of not admitting a hunch she'd had all along.

'The real borders are in people's heads. You won't find them on a map,' she used to tell the boys, as if she, Frauke, was personally in the know.

'You can do anything. As long as you let history teach you,' she spouted, in a different time, a time before history rose like a girl from a coffin, all set to do her thing for the first time.

'Has it ever struck you that all this is connected?'

That was the first question. Frauke didn't answer the therapist. She took the question home with her like a cushion to rest on.

Beat around the bush. Up until then, when it came to her breakdown, it's what people had done. Conversations about the weather mostly. It was awkward. The Irish had taught her well.

'Yes, it's raining, but what can you expect? It's an Irish summer,' she remembers hearing herself.

Um den heißen Brei herumreden.

'Talk around the hot porridge.'

Her literal translation of the German equivalent of yet another English language proverb made her chuckle, momentarily lightened the mood.

'It's how we Irish survive. We beat around the bush for a living,' Dermot said. The therapist's question about what she wanted aged eleven came next. Frauke was appalled. Going back in time while Rome is burning. Eventually, she went back in stages, stopping along the way. Hailing from a city, when she first visited Ireland in her twenties, it was the fields she loved, the rolling hills and hedgerows, the greens and browns. A simple thing to fall for, like first love. Smitten. Cattle standing peaceful under drizzle, walking slowly through gates, oblivious as to where and what end. One cool spring morning her future husband led a cow into a trailer, instantly locating the spot in the neck where the animal least felt the injection.

'Don't worry. It's a vaccine. This is a dairy farm. She's only going to a different field,' he said when her eyes welled up.

A vaccine for what? That, she didn't ask. She'd rushed into the scene, and when Dermot said that he loved her German-ness, her tendency to take things at face value, she settled, feeling needed, like a pioneer, a frontier close by. Long before that she won prizes in school. 'A reader and thinker,' her school reports said.

On bad days, with her final sick line about to run out, the devastation amounts to a needle stuck in her skin.

Considering what might be ahead of them, how dare these girls snicker and spit? *Hochmut kommt vor dem Fall.*

And still, thirty years ago, had a middle-aged woman driven past her at slow speed, Frauke, too, would have pulled a face, exaggerated, made a feast of it. *Pride comes before a fall.*

'She was staring like a cow,' she would have sneered.

The thought makes her break the speed limit, then quickly slow down again, check her face in the mirror. A cow, unsure how to be one.

There are good days, too. Days when the girls remind Frauke of things she believes to be true. She was right to walk out of that classroom.

'Every single one of these girls will have to think of herself as possible, regardless of place, language, history,' she tells Dermot.

'That's a given,' he replies, trying his best to answer back when all Frauke wants is to break open a dead end. She doesn't give out to him, though. His love, it's another thing she wants, now especially.

Sometimes the girls make her think of famous portraits. Vermeer, Da Vinci, Dürer. The same faces, time and again. History in the making. The readers and thinkers are easily spotted. They stand like sisters, each of them with blind spots, not unlike the men who painted them. It surprises her, how, thinking like this, familiarity doesn't breed contempt. Spotting the clues for common ground, she still is good at that. It's like coming back into her life through the back door, taking a closer look than before, the silence in her head like the sound of underwater during the last lap at the pool when she dives, briefly immune to her own judgment.

'Keep your wits about you.'

Einen klaren Kopf behalten.

Sometimes she wants to call to the girls. As if they need rescued. They don't. And she doesn't either. Her parents didn't stop her when she wanted to emigrate. The world didn't stop her. She knew what was happening in Ireland. She came anyway. This is how history works. If only she can keep her wits about her, lure that eleven year-old reader and thinker once more, beat around the bush until she comes out and tells her: what now?

Rowena Warwick

Rowena Warwick has a diploma in creative writing from
Oxford and an MA in creative writing from Bath Spa, both
with distinction. Her poetry is widely published and has
been placed and listed in competitions, most notably Magma
and The Hippocrates Prize. She has been longlisted for the
National Poetry Prize. Her first novel is underway. Mostly she
is writing, but when she isn't you may find her working in the
NHS or playing her trumpet.

Smoking Area

The first she knew of it was the picture of her house on the news website. It wasn't her whole house, just the driveway to the side, the hedge and a first floor window, her undrawn curtains. There was a figure standing on the gravel of her drive. She clicked to make it bigger. A policewoman.

It was definitely the pub next door too. The Flag and Thistle. Obviously it was, the headline said it all. She just had difficulty believing it, the name, it was so nice, so friendly. No one got stabbed in Weston Poyle.

'It's a good job you're away,' her brother said. She was staying with her brother overnight in the city. They were to visit their mother on the Saturday: her brother's flat was considerably closer. 'At the very least you would have heard the altercation, seen it maybe.' He leaned across and switched on the TV, the rolling news channel. It was all about leaving the EU. 'Bad timing,' he said, muting the sound. 'Are they allowed to stand on your drive, without your permission, the police?' He picked up two slices of bread, 'more toast?'

She sat with her coffee mug suspended halfway to her mouth. She put it down with a clunk, slopping the hot brown fluid. He appeared at her shoulder with a cloth. 'Whoops,' he said.

The Flag and Thistle. Right next door. Two paragraphs. A man had died and another had been taken to hospital with critical injuries, whatever that meant. The Flag and Thistle, where her daughter used to wash up when she was a teenager. It had been convenient. It paid reasonably well. Thank goodness the children were all grown up and off doing their own thing. Her husband was away too, on a business trip. Berlin. Back tomorrow. What a relief. Her brother was probably right, it was a good thing she was here in his flat, had been all night, that none of them were home.

'Oh look, here we go,' her brother said turning up the sound. 'Your house doesn't look too bad. Your hedge could do with a cut though.' He laughed. The camera panned from the pub, back over her house and onto the village green where a group of people were gathered behind a police cordon. Bunches of flowers were heaped on the wet grass in front of them. A woman in a red coat and matching lipstick held a large microphone, trying to spin out the few facts. An argument, a death, not in the pub but behind it, in the smoking area.

'Well, you could have seen it all from your bedroom window,' her brother said. She shuddered, shut her eyes. Someone's son, their brother, maybe their dad.

On the way up the motorway to her mother's bungalow she put the seat back and tried to sleep. It had been an uncomfortable night on her brother's sofa-bed but it was the routine they had got into. One Friday each month she would stay with him and the following morning they would drive to spend a few hours with their mother. They used to take her out somewhere, lunch, the coast, the shopping centre. It was harder now, mum was so much less mobile, and the last time they had visited she seemed a little confused. Her brother had packed a cool bag, they would warm up the food and dish it out themselves. He liked to cook although sometimes their mother found it a little spicy.

Despite the poor night she couldn't sleep, the road surface seemed more noisy than usual, the winter light brighter. She took out her phone. Three notifications. Her daughter on Instagram, the photo from the website. It had been annotated with two arrows, 'murder site', and 'my house', alarmingly close together. It had ten likes already. A WhatsApp from her son, 'Seen the news Mum? Anyone we know?' A winking emoji. An email from her husband, it was raining in Berlin.

After lunch her brother turned on the television, but their mother didn't have any fancy channels and it was the wrong time for the news. She checked her phone while he watched the football and her mother dozed in her high-backed armchair. The victim had been nineteen. Four men had been arrested. Perhaps it *was* someone they knew. Unlikely she thought. Her children were well into their twenties now and even if they had been at the same school it would be very unlikely their paths would have crossed. Someone's younger sibling, maybe? She hoped not. Her brother had tried to show their mother the news article, but she kept putting her finger on the screen of his phone, moving the pictures on to something else. He gave up, smiling and shaking his head.

On the way back to the city he had agreed that their mother was becoming more confused. The thought of her continuing to live alone was a problem they would have to tackle. They would both try to think about what to do, ready for the next time.

By the time she got back to Weston Poyle late the same evening, it was dark. The single streetlamp at the edge of the green sparked the occasional cellophaned glint from the grey heap of flowers on the grass.

There was a police tape across the front of the pub and a uniformed officer stood outside the door, the Flag and Thistle sign swinging above his head. Thankfully her own driveway was clear.

She sat in her silent car for a moment, looking at the black outline of the bricks which made up her garage and merged into the dividing wall between her property and the pub. It wasn't a bad pub, they'd never had any trouble, not in the fifteen years they'd lived here. It could be a little noisy at turning out time but that was to be expected. She rarely went in there, preferring the George on the other side of the green. It did quizzes for the air ambulance and had its own microbrewery. Her husband liked the craft beer. No, there was nothing much about the Flag and Thistle, it was an ordinary sort of pub, frequented by ordinary sorts of people.

She tried to get the situation into focus. There were only thirty feet or so between where she sat quietly in her car and the place where only twenty-four hours ago, a young man had met a violent death. When she opened the car door would the air feel different? Would something of him still be there? Would it have come through the wall and into her garden? She looked away, to her house, the dark of her bedroom window, the bare leaves of her climbing roses shivering against the brickwork. It was a shame no one else was home.

There was post on the mat and the still air in the hallway still carried a trace of the casserole they had eaten earlier in the week. She carried her overnight bag upstairs, dumped it on the bed, undressed and got into the shower. It was good to be back, her duty done for another month, to her brother as much as her mother. He seemed happy enough but she worried about him living on his own in his little flat. She knew she shouldn't, but he was seven years younger than her and she supposed she would always think of him as her *little* brother, the one she used to look out for. She let the water run across her body, slowly turning pink in the heat, the shower door steaming over.

Wrapped in the towel she went back into the bedroom. There was something different about the room. Usually at this time of night the voices from the pub would be tinkling, rising and falling. There would be laughing, footsteps, the clink of glasses. She had grown so accustomed to it over the years that it had become part of the bedroom, like the hollyhocks of the wallpaper. This unaccustomed silence was deep.

At the window she looked out. The customary lights of the smoking area were off, she could barely make out the line of the picnic table which was usually strewn with ashtrays, or the few chairs which littered the edges of the space. As she waited for her eyes to become accustomed to the night, a light came on in an upstairs window at the back of the pub. The smoking area jumped into the yellow glow, the uneven concrete base, the shoddy canopy. One of the chairs was on its side. She pulled the towel tighter round her. She imagined a group of lads going out the back, leaning against the table, lighting up, one of them saying something. A push, a shove, a knife. Had it been that simple? Or maybe he had already been out there, the smell of fear on him. Maybe he had been pursued, like in those horrible cases in the paper, where a gang chased some poor innocent until they were cornered like a wild animal. Or maybe it had been a rendezvous, a handover, drugs. Guns, even. But this was Weston Polye, what did people hand over here other than heritage seeds and bottles of homemade rhubarb gin?

She pulled the curtains shut, slipped her nightdress on over her head, went back to the bathroom to clean her teeth. As she looked in the mirror she wondered if her mother had gone to bed yet. She had a suspicion she was sleeping downstairs in the armchair most nights now. Her brother had shrugged at the suggestion, maybe, who knew? When they had got back to his flat there was a friend waiting for him, on the sofa with a can of beer in his hand. Her brother had seemed embarrassed, hurried her out and on her way home. On the journey she had felt sad, sad that her mother was old and wouldn't always be there, sad that her brother didn't trust her with the details of his life. And now she was home she couldn't shake the feeling, as if suddenly the world had become very subdued.

She flicked off the bedroom light and turned back the duvet. The chink of light from the pub window was coming through the gap in the curtains casting a yellow line across her pillow. It would stop her sleeping.

She grasped the edges of the curtains but before she could pull them together the light outside disappeared. She could see something was moving low in the smoking area, by the bins. The dark sweep of a fox nosed in the trail of litter, moved on. From the shadows a man stepped silently across the empty space. He stopped at the picnic table, swung his leg through the gap and sat down. She watched as he held a flicker in his hand, felt him breathe in, the hot red tip of his cigarette expanding between his lips.

Christopher Young

Christopher Young is a writer based in Southwark, South London. His fiction has been published in *T-R-E-M-O-R-S* magazine, and he has been longlisted for the Bath Novel Award. In 2014, he received the Malcolm Bradbury Continuation Prize for Prose Fiction from the University of East Anglia. He is currently working on his first novel, about inequality and class in the service industry.

Centre

We met outside the E.L. centre. Six kids were gathered on their bikes outside the Chinese supermarket, which was in between the Syrian café and the bookies. Taken as one the shop fronts looked like a flag: yellow, red, green. On the other corner, the charity shop was closed. Two women slept in a tent under the lime tree. The kids weren't going anywhere, they didn't look in a hurry. They had matching grey tracksuits, bikes with boosted tyres. A young couple walked past pushing a pram, followed by two old men and a dog. Newspapers scattered like crabs crossing the sea floor. The wind was sweet with petrol and the sky was stretched out thin above the E.L. towers, which had been scorched black by the air. Time slipped, a door to the Chinese supermarket opened and one kid in a puffa ran out, so they all hit their bikes and started spinning spokes, laughing until they were out of reach. The shopkeeper cursed and called out past the roundabout and kept shouting down the bus lane but she didn't give chase. She stood staring for minutes after they were gone, then turned inside. The day died and the E.L. sign snapped on in royal blue. Against the night, the lights switched on in the towers in staggered bursts, as if they were just now waking up. The lights came on in the South Tower, then the North.

We met outside the E.L. centre. Rain fell, doubling the shop fronts in the pavement. A brass band played a sitcom theme outside the charity shop, a hat half-full of coins in front of them. The kids were back, this time sheltering in the alley between the bookies and the charity shop. The kid with the puffa was leaning back against his bike, which had scratched-up blue rims. His trainers had orange laces. He was quiet, and his friends were joking around him. A businessman pocketed his glasses, entered the bookies, left after a few minutes and lit a cigarette. The window displayed their most attractive odds. Music was coming from the Syrian place, we could hear it when the brass band took a break.

We met outside the E.L. centre. Buses were backed up bumper to bumper, and school kids waved from one top deck to the next. A woman walked three girls in blue blazers into the Syrian café, their hair braided with pink and orange. She came out with three coffees and let the girls drop them off in front of the tent. TVs flickered inside the bookies, and two of the kids walked past without their bikes. A teenager hauled box after box of preserves into the Chinese supermarket while his boss watched from behind the counter, smoking a cigarette. The air was light and dry, as if the cold had sucked it inside out.

We met outside the E.L. centre. There were large cracks in both of the windows of the Syrian café. The café was still open, and the owner was sat in front with a small brown cup of something. One of the women was out of the tent with her dog. She had tracksuits that only just hung on to her, but her dog looked well-fed and happy. She shouted something at the kids as they rode past, but they ignored her and pulled up by the café. The owner raised his hand in greeting, and they asked him what had happened, but he only shook his head. Later the shopkeeper from the Chinese supermarket came out for a smoke and the kids departed. The lights came on in the towers, first the South Tower, then the North.

We met outside the E.L. centre. Carollers were outside the charity shop, singing Silent Night, while the women from the tent were sat outside with the dog. They were doing a brisk trade, and had each been given something hot in styrofoam cups. They were all in their twenties. The Syrian café had taped up the cracks on its windows, and the kid with the orange laces walked past, dressed in a suit for church.

We made our way past the E.L. centre. It was boxed off from the street by police tape. The shops were closed and the tent had been moved. The lights came on in the towers, first the South Tower, then the North.

We made our way past the E.L. centre. The tape had been taken down and the centre was busy again, washed in pale sun. Two toddlers ran in and out of the Chinese supermarket as the owner watched them and laughed. A woman in a long jacket held a microphone and spoke into it under the lime tree, as someone else operated a large, heavy camera. Passers by stopped to watch. A businessman stepped out of the bookies, saw the cameras, and went back in. People were filming them filming on their phones. After a few minutes the woman put away her microphone and started writing something on a clipboard. The one with the camera went over to get a close-up of the wreaths that had been laid outside the charity shop.

We made our way past the E.L. centre. The kids were back but there weren't so many of them. The air was thick and warm as wool but they were still dressed in all-black tracksuits and hoods. The bark of the tree was criss-crossed by small canyons, its leaves were shaped like hearts.

We made our way past the E.L. centre. A mural had appeared on the wall to the right of the charity shop. Electric blue, pink, green waves crashed around a serious face with wide open eyes: the kid with orange laces. Beneath his face they had written his name, his age, a prayer.

We made our way past the E.L. centre. Up on the towers, satellite dishes stared at each other with blank faces across hot, shivering air. Transmissions hummed above, data pinballed, white noise filling space like smoke. A man was asleep at the bottom of the lime tree, using his fist as a pillow. The shop windows were filled with brassy light. The manager of the Chinese supermarket came out for a cigarette, her arm in a sling. She watched as a kid sprinted into the alleyway between the bookies and the charity shop and disappeared. A minute later a police car pulled up, shining silver-yellow-blue. Two policemen ran into the shadows and reemerged with the boy in a headlock. One of them was holding a net over the boy's head, pulling him down to the ground. They flattened him and knelt on his back. The manager walked towards them, shouting, but they shoved her and she fell to her backside, unable to break her fall with her arm. Faces appeared at windows. The policemen picked the boy up by his arms and legs, and his shirt rode up and exposed his stomach. They dropped him in the backseat, and removed the net from over his face.

We made our way past the E.L. centre. Two men in high-visibility jackets were sawing through the limbs of the lime tree, filling the air with dust. The glass panes at the front of the Syrian café had been replaced. In front of the mural of the boy a man was speaking through a megaphone. He wore a suit and had a gleaming shaved head. Next to him three young men were holding up a large, limp flag. Passers-by peeled off to watch and film on their phones, and a small crowd gathered. Some people shouted at him in passing, another person spat on the ground. The police were called, but they stood back and watched the crowd as he spoke. The owner of the Syrian café stepped out and watched for a few minutes, then stepped back inside. The man who slept under the tree had been moved, so that he wasn't hit by falling branches. Only some of the lights worked in the E.L. centre sign, and it now said only CENTRE, bold and blue.

We made our way past the E.L. centre. Rain hammered the pavement, splashing upwards at people's ankles. The man in the suit had returned, except this time his crowd was much bigger, with many people carrying flags and placards. Fluorescent police vests surrounded them like a bracelet. Another, larger, crowd had been drawn in protest, with their own banners and placards. The man spoke through his megaphone, inaudible under chant after chant. Two kids watched in silence from up in the naked branches of the tree. The day was shorter but the heat lingered beneath the rain. The crowds pressed together and split apart again, together, apart. They moved like a school of fish feeding, only the thin line of police separating the two.

We made our way past the E.L. centre. The sky was a rock pool, dark and deep at the North Tower, shallow and pristine at the South Tower. Gulls spent the day in the inbetween, banking against the wind, hanging still. The windows of the Syrian café had been smashed open again, and the insides of the building blackened by fire. The Chinese supermarket had been broken into and torched. There was glass, soot, and silver packages of food scattered across the pavement, and the mural had been crossed out in white paint. The bookies escaped with the windows intact, and the lime tree still stood.

We moved in near the E.L. centre. The streets were quiet, and the bus routes had been diverted somewhere else. The shops were closed, boarded up with plywood except for the bookies. Their TVs were shining racecourse green. Three men slept under the tree in foetal positions. A dog's head peeked out of a sleeping bag, also asleep.

We moved in near the E.L. centre. The air was heavy and sour, hard to breathe, as the sun rose white as a bulb behind thick cloud. Airplanes queued up into the distance. The lights turned off in the South Tower, then the North. Ariels quivered in the open. Under the tree, the men and the dog were asleep, arranged under their sleeping bags. A crowd of onlookers grew through the morning, and two camera crews set up, along with another team of police. The crowd were all young and smartly dressed, wearing masks for the pollution. After midday, when the sky was white as bone, a tall, handsome man gave a speech in front of the shut-down café. Behind him was a wide blue banner with short, friendly slogans. He had a white shirt on, unbuttoned to his chest, and his crowd applauded whenever he wasn't speaking. There was sweat on his brow and in patches on his back and chest.

We moved in near the E.L. centre. Fog sat on top of the shops. A businessman walked up to the bookies, pretended to receive a phone call, and turned away at the door.

We moved in near the E.L. centre. There was a line of police vans and construction workers outside the South Tower. A woman in a nightgown was leaning out of her third-storey window, shouting at the police below. One of them was talking to her through a loudspeaker, but she kept shouting over it. She disappeared inside for a moment then returned with a dinner plate and threw it to the ground, just missing the crowd. Minutes later a group of police disappeared up into the building. Under the tree two of the men were awake and sat by their sleeping bags, while the other had disappeared with his dog. A businessman left the bookies and lit a cigarette, then squatted down to talk to them. The lights came on in the South Tower, then the North.

We moved in near the E.L. centre. It was morning and the centre was deserted: the bookies were closed, the men had moved on with their sleeping bags, and the traffic had been diverted. Birds refused to pass between the towers. The sky was a chemical pink, and the breeze heavy and close, smelling of diesel and spilled ink. The lights were off in the tower a little earlier than usual. A loudspeaker could be heard in the distance, and then three long, loud digital tones. Silence resettled for an instant and then both towers cracked a third of the way up. Dark bouquets of dust spun out into the air. The towers teetered, black insides spilling from their middles, then keened towards one another, folding against and into themselves, and collapsed. The sound of brick on brick echoed out across the streets, across the causeway, across the train tracks, across our homes. The cloud was visible for miles until, by degrees, the wind bore it away.

We moved in near the E.L. centre. The brass band played carols in front of the charity shop, as people stopped and bent to give them some change. A woman came from inside the shop carrying a tray of hot drinks. She distributed them to the men sleeping under the tree, and they nodded their thanks. The kids were back in the alleyway, crowded around a phone. The towers were gone but the air still smelled of everything that had spilled out from inbetween the apartments, stairwells and floors.

We moved in near the E.L. centre. Snow fell and disappeared the instant it hit the pavement. The buses were passing again, but less frequently. There was a tent in the alleyway with one man in it, wearing a mask for the pollution. Under the lime tree one woman was asleep with a fat, white mongrel on a leash, while another person filled a sleeping bag, barely visible, with only their scalp showing. Two kids walked past them in pressed dark trousers, rucksacks and puffa jackets. They slipped into the alley between the bookies and the charity shop. The facades of the Syrian café and the Chinese supermarket had been replaced, this time with large colourful boards advertising retail space. On one board a woman was choosing a handbag from a rack of three, while on the other two men sat down for coffee. The boards spoke of square feet, of transport links, of an up-and-coming area for professionals. They gave a phone number and an email address. The bookies' windows had been replaced with the same messaging. Each shop had been painted over in white, so they were no longer yellow, red and green. All over the charity shop windows, again and again, large blue letters spelled out COMING SOON.

Judges' Profiles

Billy Kahora (Chair)

Billy is lecturer in Creative and Professional Writing at Bristol University. His short stories have been published in *Chimurenga*, *McSweeney's*, Granta Online, *Internazionale*, *Vanity Fair* and *Kwani*. He was shortlisted for the Caine Prize for African Literature in 2012 and 2014. He has been editor of the *Kwani Journal* and has run writing workshops for a decade. His debut short story collection, *The Cape Cod Bicycle War* was published in 2019.

Sharmaine Lovegrove

Sharmaine founded, and is publisher at, Dialogue Books, part of the world's second biggest publishing group, Hachette. Dialogue focus on publishing writers often under-represented and overlooked by mainstream publishers. Previously, Sharmaine ran an English language bookshop in Berlin for several years, and has also been a literary scout, and Literary Editor of *Elle* magazine. She was named *The Bookseller* magazine's FutureBook Person of the Year in 2018, and co-founded the Black Writers' Guild in 2020.

Anneliese Mackintosh

Anneliese's short story collection, *Any Other Mouth*, won the Green Carnation Prize. It was also shortlisted for the Edge Hill Prize, Saltire Society's First Book Award, and the Saboteur Awards, and longlisted for the Frank O'Connor International Short Story Award. Her debut novel, *So Happy It Hurts*, was shortlisted for a DIVA Rising Star Award. Anneliese's short fiction has been broadcast on BBC Radio 4, BBC Radio Scotland and published in many magazines and anthologies. She has a PhD in Creative Writing and her third novel, *Bright and Dangerous Objects*, was published in 2020.

Tom Robinson

Tom has been a bookseller and bookshop manager for the last twelve years, and is currently the manager of Foyles in Bristol. He first started working in the cookery section of the Waterstones in Wimbledon Bridge, and will likely still attempt to tell you about the qualities of Lebanese cuisine if given the chance. Between 2008 and 2013, Tom co-edited *Rattle: A Journal at the Convergence of Art and Writing*. Short stories and novellas have always represented a significant portion of Tom's reading habits, and in general he would prefer reading lots of little books to fewer big ones.

Acknowledgements

Enormous thanks to the following people for their vital contributions and support for this year's Bristol Short Story Prize:

The judging panel: Billy Kahora, Sharmaine Lovegrove, Anneliese Mackintosh and Tom Robinson. Our readers: Georgia Bate, Diane Becker, Jo Borek, Jo Darque, Lu Hersey, Sandra Hopkins, Jeanette Jarvie, Richard Jones, Mike Manson, Bertel Martin, Catherine Mason, Eva Mason, Dawn Pomroy, Pam Smallwood.

Chris Hill, Jonathan Ward, Roisin Oakley and the 3rd year Illustration students at the University of the West of England. Professors Helen Fulton and Mary Luckhurst at Bristol University. Tangent Books; Foyles; Peter Morgan and Mark Furneval at ScreenBeetle; Bristol 24/7; and Joe Burt, Nicky Coates, Andy Hamilton, Rosa Lovegood, Louis Melia, Natasha Melia, Dave Oakley, Lisa Price, and Thomas Rasche.

Biggest and most heartfelt thanks go to all the writers who submitted their stories to the 2020 Bristol Short Story Prize in what has been such an extreme time for all. It has been a very uplifting and moving process to read, share, debate and discuss so many wonderful stories.

2020
Bristol Short Story
Prize Longlist

(a-z by writer's name)

Arif Anwar	*Pig*
Samuel Atkins	*Today was Tuesday*
Andre Bagoo	*Simple Things*
Erika Banerji	*Marvellous Real*
Jo Beckett-King	*The Croft*
Ella Bradshaw	*The Living*
Ethan Chapman	*Where Have All the Children Gone?*
Chelsea Chong	*This is Not a Drill*
Bethan Cooke	*Stopping Point*
Habiba Cooper Diallo	*Desert Blues*
Tessa Duell	*Man's Best Friend*
Fiona Ennis	*Host*
Carol Farrelly	*Clipped*
Laura Freeman	*One Last Look*
Steven Fromm	*Six Carp*
Chris Gates	*Weaver's Trap*
Faiza Hasan	*A Tapestry of Flowers*
David Shelley Jones	*Six Foot Track*

2020 Bristol Short Story Prize Longlist

Lubnaa Joomun	*A Dance with the Wind*
Radhika Kapur	*The School Play*
Olivia Katrandjian	*The Children Shall Be Spared*
Sarah Burton Kennedy	*How to Prolong Your Existence*
Barbara Leahy	*The Time It Takes to Smoke a Cigarette*
Tehila Lieberman	*Bedtime Story*
Niamh MacCabe	*Hex: A Self Instructs Itself*
Faraaz Mahomed	*1993*
Wah Mak	*Old Crush on the 703*
Michael Mau	*Pal*
Stephen Narain	*What In Me Is Dark, Illumine*
Gamuchirai Nhengu	*Normal Girl*
Will Neal	*Interdependence*
Makena Onjerika	*Girl Games*
Heenali Patel	*Onwards*
Natalie Serrag	*Fish*
Honor Somerset	*The Jesus Tree*
Susanne Stich	*Unmappable*
Valerie Trapp	*Eve*
Rowena Warwick	*Smoking Area*
Andrea Watts	*Stone Flowers*
Christopher Young	*Centre*

Winner of the 2020 Sansom Award for Bristol Writers:

Joe Wedgbury   *A Lady on the 'Dog*

Notable Contenders: (these stories were in the running for the longlist until the final decisions were made)

Ali Al-Jamri	*The Forecast from Jau Prison*
Alan Bern	*Twinzed*
Annalisa Crawford	*One Minute Silence*
John Etcheverry	*Speck*
Aidan Furey	*Vernon Montgomery is Not Dead*
Bhavika Govil	*Naan Bread*
Raphaela Hopson	*Rinse. Eat. Bathe. Repeat.*
Christian Livermore	*Bluet*
Conn Redden	*Gomoecca*
Dierdre Shanahan	*Overnight in the Day Room*
Anna Stewart	*Floors Spread Cold*